Dedicated to my daughter, Megan,

and to anyone else who has been involved

in an abusive relationship.

All proceeds from the sale of this book will be donated to Safe

Passage to support its programs addressing intimate partner

violence. To learn more, visit safepass.org.

Acknowledgements

To Megan Pehoviak, Wilbraham & Monson Academy Class of 2014, for providing expert nursing questions.

To Wendy Notarnicola, of Blue Note Editing & Writing, for her professional editing.

To my cousin's daughter, Adina Taylor, for drawing a wonderful cover design – again!!!

To my mom, Joan Wells, for proofreading 52,000 words in two days while visiting for Christmas of 2018.

To all of my friends, for their continued support.

And to my family, for letting me do what I do.

Chapter 1

The red three-ring binders were perfectly aligned along the four rows of the dust-free, oak bookshelf. White horizontal stickers displayed the years, written by hand in blue ink dating back to 1970.

"There's an index at the start of each book," Ken Roy said. "Every customer we have ever had is in these binders. Tell the new person everything they'll need is right in here."

"We know all about your books, Mr. Roy. No one kept better records than you," Kevin Huber said.

"*Keeps*. I'm not out the door yet."

"When did my grandfather hire you? 1940?"

"It was '70, wise guy," retorted Ken, who began working at Huber Heating and Air Conditioning two days after he graduated high school. "You know that. I owe everything I have to your grandfather. He paved the way for me."

"He would say you paved your own way and I would agree with him. You care more about our company than we do, and we own the place."

"It was a great place to work for forty-seven-plus years. I got to work most of my life with my best friend, your dad, God rest his soul."

"He loved working with you, Mr. Roy. Growing up he always said we were lucky to have you as an employee. I never understood what he was talking about; I was just a kid. But I understand now. There's no way we can replace you. I feel badly for the new guy, and he's my friend. I know he has some experience, but no one can manage an office and personnel like you."

"I enjoyed it. That was the key. I enjoyed coming to work every day."

'Mr. Roy, can you help me with one last thing?"

"I thought I showed you everything? Did I miss something?"

"Nope, you didn't miss anything. I just need help with one thing before we end the day."

The two men, a generation apart, walked out of Ken's small office into the lobby. The company's staff of six stood smiling, and Kevin's wife, Doreen, held a round cheesecake, already cut into eight slices.

"Mr. Roy, I know you told me not to get you anything, but we couldn't let you just walk out the door on your last day without doing something," said Doreen, her voice quivering slightly. "Forty-seven years is a long time."

"Oh, you guys didn't have to do anything. I'd rather just keep working and leave at the end of the day, just like always."

"Yes, we know, but that just didn't seem right today," replied Doreen with an uncomfortable smile.

"Speech!" said Chuck Wallace, a 25-year technician at the company.

"Speech! Speech!" echoed Chuck's twin brother, Larry.

"Yeah, Mr. Roy. Say a few words," Kevin said with a smile.

"Ahhh, not my style; but if that's what you want, Kevin, I will. You're the boss."

Ken looked down, put both hands in his pockets, and rocked slightly back-and-forth.

"OK, so without giving this much thought ... um, I wish Marie was here. She would know what I should say."

Kevin pursed his lips together and Doreen, already on edge, started to get teary-eyed. The other employees maintained their fixed gaze on Ken as he searched for words.

"I received an opportunity a long time ago. Mr. Huber, Kevin's grandfather, was generous to think of me when he opened this business. He was a great man. I respected him. Um ... "

Everyone stood perfectly still as Ken paused.

"I'm really not good at this. I'm not one to give speeches. I guess what I want to tell you is that I enjoyed working with all of you, and I'm sure you'll do great things without me. This company has been around a long time."

"Yeah, and you've been here for that entire time," Kevin interjected. "I won't beat around the bush, Mr. Roy. I'm nervous; we're all nervous. No one knows this company better than you. No one. Part of me does want to keep you on part-time, and I know you'd like to do that, but in my heart I know that would be selfish of me. You've put in almost five decades of service. It's time for you to retire. It won't be easy, and my guess is that we'll have some bumps in the road, but we'll have to adjust to life without Ken Roy here at Huber."

"You'll be fine, and you know how to reach me if anything pops up."

"Mr. Roy, since we're all together, and I know I speak for everyone here, I'd like to say that you have been a role model for all of us," said Doreen, her voice cracking and trailing off. "Sorry. You're such a gentleman."

"Thank you, Doreen. Everyone, thank you."

Other than Doreen's whimpers, the staff remained respectfully silent. Ken was either a friend or father figure to everyone at the company.

"OK, enough of this. Let's eat some cake. You picked out my favorite, Doreen. Thank you."

The slender forty-year-old put the cheesecake on the nearest desk. She pulled some spoons and paper plates out of a plastic bag wrapped around her right wrist before carefully tugging each piece off of the round base and onto the plates.

Methodically, Doreen handed Ken a piece of his favorite dessert.

"You first, Mr. Roy."

Chapter 2

The brown box contained fourteen framed photographs – one for every employee who had worked at Huber's during Ken's time at the company.

"Do you want to take anything else?" Kevin asked.

"Nope. The rest is company supplies," said Ken, who held the box easily with both hands. "I just want the pictures. I'm changing my wife's sewing room into a reading room, and the photos will be good for me. I'll always be surrounded by my friends."

"Here, let me get the front door for you."

Kevin slipped between Ken and a desk before hustling to the door. As he pulled it open, the bell at the top jingled.

"Thanks, Kevin."

Ken shifted the box to his left hip, opened the passenger door and placed the box on the front seat. Then he closed the door and stuck his hand out toward Kevin.

"Call if you need anything."

"I'm going to do my best to *not* call," Kevin replied as the two men shook hands. "You deserve some peace and quiet."

"Yeah, peace and quiet."

"Would you like to come over for Easter dinner in a few weeks?"

"Maybe. Thanks for the offer, Kevin. I haven't thought that far ahead yet."

"I understand. Well, we'll save you a seat. You're welcome at our home anytime."

"OK. Thanks."

"Bye, Mr. Roy."

Ken nodded as he opened the door to his silver Toyota Camry and started the engine. Kevin raised his right hand and waved as the company's final founding member drove out of the parking lot at dusk.

Chapter 3

Ken flicked up the light switch with his left elbow, and the tall lamp in the left corner illuminated the small room upstairs. He searched for the best place to put the box of photos before stepping forward and putting them on the floor under the window. Standing erect again, he looked at his wife's sewing machine, and then, above it, at the only decoration on the walls – a family photograph of Ken, his wife, Marie, and their daughter,

Brooke, at a Boston Red Sox game in 2004. The field and Fenway Park's Green Monster were in the background.

"I guess that one can stay," Ken said before walking out of the room and down the stairs.

He sat in his recliner in the family room, electing not to pull the wooden lever. He gently rocked back-and-forth. A few minutes passed.

"Sweetheart," Ken said in a normal tone.

Ken heard a propeller airplane fly overhead, the low hum fading slowly into silence. Ken used the balls of his feet to move the chair ever so slightly forward and back.

"Sweetheart. This is going to be harder than I thought. I'm bored already."

A car drove by, prompting Ken to look toward the picture window and the darkness that was settling in for the evening. He lowered his eyes a notch, to where his wife's wheelchair was placed squarely toward the window. He stared, recalling the day four months earlier when the wheelchair first entered the house.

###

"Sweetheart, do you want to stop somewhere on the way home to get anything?" Ken asked as he pushed Marie toward the car through a coating of November snow in the parking lot of Pynchonton Hospital.

Marie groaned. The Amyotrophic Lateral Sclerosis (ALS) had taken away her ability to speak. The debilitating disease had also stripped her of her ability to stand eight months after her initial diagnosis.

"OK, we'll go straight home. It's cold, and it's supposed to start snowing again, too. Looks like we'll have a white Thanksgiving."

The couple drove home, with Ken hurrying to the vehicle's trunk to grab the wheelchair. He opened Marie's door and slipped his hands underneath her armpits, with his chest to her back. He pulled Marie, twisting his hips and adjusting his feet as he fluidly plopped Marie into the wheelchair.

"Hey, that was easy. We can handle that."

Marie groaned.

"You're welcome."

Ken rolled his wife of nearly forty-six years up the cement walkway to the front door, where he turned the chair around and hip-checked the door as he backed inside.

"Our first day with the wheelchair and we've got this down," he happily said as he pushed Marie into the family room. "I moved a few things a little bit so we can wheel your chair easily in and out of the room."

Ken positioned the wheelchair so that Marie was centered in front of the picture window, leaving enough room so her tan slippers didn't brush up against the wall.

"Do you need anything, Sweetheart?" Ken asked.

Marie bobbed her head side-to-side. The weight of it made it look more like her head was bouncing.

"OK. I'm going to go cut some of those branches in the front yard so you can see the neighborhood better. You can watch. It's not exactly like watching the Bruins, but we can watch them tonight. They play Montreal at seven."

Ken leaned forward, turned his shoulders and gave his wife a soft kiss on her forehead. He smiled.

"I'll come check on you in a half hour. Well, you know how I get going sometimes, so maybe it will be an hour."

After a stroke of her shoulder-length brown hair, Ken left the room and went into the garage.

Ken stood slowly and hesitated before moving with a purpose toward the picture window. He grabbed the wheelchair by the handles and rolled it out of the room and through the kitchen to the door leading to the garage. He folded the chair and opened the door, carefully maneuvering down the two steps. He leaned the wheelchair against the large blue trash container and stepped back.

"Used it for less than two months."

Ken stood motionless in the garage, staring at the empty, folded wheelchair. The seconds passed before he looked down, noticing some pebbles on the gray concrete floor. He turned and grabbed the dustpan and brush hanging along the wall to the left of the workbench. As he bent down he saw more pebbles - a trail, in fact, leading out of the garage. He realized the dirt must have been on the wheels when he brought the trash container inside while it was raining the previous day.

Industrial broom in hand, he began sweeping the dirt trail, then the entire garage, then the entire driveway, and the sidewalk in front of his white, split-level home. When he finished the sidewalk, he picked up the sticks along the tree belt, wandering into the road in the darkness to grab even the smallest pieces of wood.

The clock on the black-faced microwave read 8:57 p.m. when he walked into the kitchen. He made his favorite sandwich – turkey on white bread with yellow mustard and a thin layer of mayonnaise – and sat in his recliner.

"I think they're on," said Ken, grabbing the clicker with his left hand.

After the push of a button, the Boston Celtics appeared on the television screen. Ken settled into his chair, content with his efforts for the evening. He watched the game before dozing off, a white plate and the clicker resting on the end table to his left and the TV still on, just as he had done every night for the last ten weeks.

Chapter 4

Day after day, Ken's routine was the same. Up early, he'd either run or ride the stationary bike for ninety minutes before meticulously tackling chores. Mowing, hedge trimming, gardening, painting, house cleaning, and any other fix-it-up job that needed to be done, Ken did it with precision.

The weekends offered a bit of a change, as Ken would drive to Pynchonton Park to jog with some running friends. Ken still had his running legs, and he enjoyed challenging himself with either a brisk pace or a long run on Saturday with friends. Afterwards, it was back home for more upkeep. Sundays were similar, with an in-and-out trip to the same church he had attended his entire life taking up his morning before accomplishing whatever task he had planned for the day. He didn't mind; it kept him moving.

The nights, though, were difficult. Sandwiches sufficed for dinner, and he could usually find one of the Boston sports team on TV. He read non-fiction when games weren't on, but he found it difficult to concentrate. His mind constantly wandered to thoughts of Marie. They had met in high school; Ken was one year older. They married a year after Marie graduated high school, when Ken had already finished two years at Huber. When their daughter and only child, Brooke, left for college in Florida, Marie began working at Huber as a secretary. They worked together for twelve years before the ALS made work tasks unbearable and unrealistic for Marie. In late 2017, she passed away.

Within an eleven-month period, Ken retired from the only place he had ever worked, lost his childhood friend and boss, Dan Huber, and watched his wife succumb to the world's most common motor neuron disease. The two people who knew him best were gone. He was friends or at least friendly with thousands of people, dating back to kindergarten in his lifelong hometown of Riversville, Massachusetts. There was only one person remaining, however, who drove him; who gave him purpose; who instilled in him an inner peace.

Chapter 5

Dinga-linga-ling; dinga-linga-ling.

"Hello?"

"Hi, Daddy."

Ken smiled, just as he did every time he heard his daughter's voice.

"Hi, Sweetie. Thanks for calling."

Brooke lived in a suburb outside of Jacksonville, Florida, with her husband of nearly two years, James Roland. The couple had a six-month old daughter, Celina.

"No problem, Daddy. Sorry I didn't come up for your retirement party."

"That's OK. Plus, it wasn't much of a party, which is the way I wanted it."

"Yeah, I know, but I wanted to be there and felt bad I wasn't able to come. I wanted to see you and everyone in the office, but it's just such a busy time at school."

"You're a working mother. That's the hardest job in the world. You don't stop."

"Yeah, I know, but I felt bad."

"How's my big girl doing?"

"She's great. She's already standing."

"Ha. She'll be running around in no time."

"So, Daddy, I'm sorry, I can't talk long tonight but I want to know how you're doing? Are you staying busy?"

"Oh, I stay busy. The house has never looked better. I don't vacuum or dust like your mother would do every week, but I'm not bored."

"That's good. I see the Bruins and Celtics are doing well."

"Yup, I watch them whenever they're on TV. I know all their names and numbers."

"Great. Well, I have to go, Daddy. James is done giving Celina her bath and I need to get her ready for bed."

"OK, Sweetie. Thanks for calling."

"Sure thing, Daddy. I'll be up in May, as soon as school is done – about ten weeks. They get done so early in the South."

"Can't wait."

"OK, love you, Daddy."

"Love you, Sweetie. Bye-bye."

"Bye."

Ken hung up the phone and walked from the kitchen to the unlit family room, purposefully lowering himself into his recliner. He turned to his left, where his wife's maroon chair-and-a-half was positioned nearby. He shifted his eyes toward the darkness on the other side of the picture window.

"Ten weeks."

Gently tapping his fingertips together, he leaned forward, maintaining his look toward his abyss.

"It's going to be a long ten weeks."

Chapter 6

The gold metal chair was placed in the mulch, centered in front of the picture window. Ken stepped up, with blue cleaning fluid in one hand and paper towels in the other. Spray and wipe; spray and wipe. He moved the chair in front of the other first floor windows, the extension ladder already standing in the driveway and propped up against the house to reach the second floor windows.

Ken felt a chill and turned toward the sky. A low rumble of thunder growled in the distance.

"Uh-oh."

The sky answered in a baritone voice.

"I guess that's it for today."

Ken tucked the towels under his left arm and grabbed the chair with his right hand.

A crack screamed from above. Ken hustled into the garage and a fat raindrop landed on the black pavement just as he reached cover. *Plop. Plop-plop-plop. Whooshhhhh.* The downpour came.

"Nuts," said Ken, noticing the ladder up against the house. Another crack rang from the sky as Ken stepped outside and grabbed the metal ladder, stepping back and lowering it horizontally before moving into the protection of the garage.

"Not smart; not smart."

Even though he had only been outside a matter of seconds, the water dripped from Ken's face. He wiped his face with a paper towel before pausing, his hands covering his face.

Dinga-linga-ling he heard faintly. In two quick steps he had opened the door and was inside the kitchen.

Dinga-linga-ling.

"Hello?"

"Mr. Roy?" the voice on the other end of the phone asked.

"Yes."

"This is Jada at Dr. Walsh's office. Are you OK?"

"Yeah. Why do ask?"

"It's not like you to miss an appointment."

"Miss an appointment?"

"Yes. You were supposed to come in for your annual appointment."

"I was?"

"Yes. Today at eight. You made the appointment a year ago when you and your wife came in. I gave her the card. I remember because she was wearing a checkered scarf that I loved."

"Oh. I, ahh, OK. Appointment today, huh?"

"Yes. But I already talked to Dr. Walsh and he said you don't have to come in if you don't want. He knows how active you are. He said if you don't want to come in, that's fine, but you have to go to the hospital to get some blood drawn."

"Blood drawn?"

"Yes, that's the best way for us to make sure you're healthy."

"OK. Can I come in today?"

"Oh, I'm sorry, we're booked solid the rest of the day, and then we're actually closing down for two weeks while we move across the street to a new building."

"Oh."

"But you can go to Pynchonton Hospital. That's where we send the results anyway. You don't need an appointment, and since it's pouring out, you probably wouldn't have to wait if you went soon. You wouldn't believe how many people don't go out in the rain."

The rain dripped from Ken's hair onto his face. A small puddle formed on the white-tiled floor around his worn sneakers.

"You don't say," he replied, shaking the water from his right arm. "OK, I'll get to the hospital today."

"OK, Mr. Roy. I'll call you back with the results when I get them."

Chapter 7

Putting the car in park, Ken looked at the windshield, which was clear of rain.

"Perfect timing," he thought.

Weaving in and out of cars as he walked through the parking lot at the hospital, Ken made his way toward the main entrance. The glass double doors opened as he approached. A chest-high, semi-circular desk appeared on the right, where a lanky, white-haired man, who looked older than Ken, stood smiling.

"Can I help you, young man?" he asked.

"I don't get called *that* every day."

"Ha! Yup, you're young to me. Everybody is."

"I'm here for some blood work."

"Vampire room. Straight down that hall. Go to the very end; last door on the right. You'll see people with fangs wearing black capes and speaking in Transylvanian accents. You might not come out."

Ken smirked as he stepped away from the desk.

"I'll let you know if I live or not," Ken said.

The gentleman winked, nodded and waved as Ken headed down the hall. He opened the door and was greeted before it closed.

"Hi! Here for blood work?"

Looking up, he saw a young Hispanic receptionist standing there, with a smile that was made for magazine covers. She had long brown hair with blonde highlights, and she was well into her third trimester of pregnancy.

"Hi. Yes, I'm here for blood work. Just an annual checkup."

"OK, just fill out this form, front and back, and then I'll take you in when you're ready. OK, Cutie?"

"Cutie? I haven't been called that in a while."

"You? I bet you're a big lady's man."

"Lady's man?" repeated Ken, shaking his head as he sat down.

Ken filled out the form, carefully checking all of the boxes. The receptionist came out from behind the desk just as he finished.

"OK, Cutie. Come with me."

She held the door open for him as he walked through the doorway and down a short hall.

"Go right in that door on the left."

Ken turned and walked into the room, sitting down in the only chair.

"Do you exercise?" the receptionist asked.

"Yup, I run or bike six days a week."

"You look like a runner. You fast?"

"Once upon a time."

The receptionist laughed as she completed a form and left it on the one table in the room.

"Well, I bet you're still fast. Stay here, Cutie. The nurse will be right in."

As soon as the receptionist left the room, a nurse came in. She was young, looking fresh out of nursing school. She stuck her hand out and smiled.

"Hi, Mr. Roy. I'm Fiona. I'm going to take your blood today. OK?"

"Hi, Fiona. Sure. Do what you have to do."

"Thanks. Go ahead and take your coat off and I'll have you out of here in no time."

The nurse prepared the needle as Ken took his coat off and hung it on the hook on the back of the door. She swabbed Ken's arm and gave it a few taps."

"There's a good one. Little pinch."

Ken watched as the needle went into his skin and the blood was sucked up into the tube.

"Did you watch? Most people don't watch."

"Yeah, I watched. It's just a little blood."

"You must have a strong stomach. Are you a doctor?"

"Air conditioning and heating."

"OK, well, you have a strong stomach," said Fiona as she put a Band-Aid on Ken's arm. "You can put your coat back on now. It's a slow day, so we'll have these results to your doctor soon. Probably today."

"Wow. Thanks."

"You're welcome."

"Fiona, can I ask you a little bit of an odd question?"

"Of course."

"Everyone here is so nice."

"I'm sorry?"

"Everyone here is so nice. The guy at the front desk, the lady who met me when I came in, you."

"Yeah, it's a nice place to work. We know no one wants to be here. We just try to make everyone as comfortable as possible. You know, just take the edge off."

"Well, mission accomplished."

"Thank you. You're so nice. You'd fit right in here."

"Well, I'm a little old to go back to school to become a doctor. Maybe in my next lifetime."

"Oh, you're too funny."

"OK, thanks. Have a nice rest of your day."

"Bye."

Ken walked out of the small room.

"Bye, Cutie," said the smiling receptionist.

"Bye," Ken beamed.

Ken left the room and turned down the hallway, walking with a bounce in his step toward the front desk. The gentleman saw Ken coming and gave him a big wave.

"Hey, you're alive," the man said in a slightly louder tone before covering his mouth with his hand. "Whoops, I probably shouldn't say that in a hospital. What do the kids say? My bad?"

Ken smiled and nodded as he stood at the front desk. He noticed a white piece of paper taped to the wooden top. He cocked his head to the left in an attempt to read it straight on.

"What's this?" Ken asked.

"Volunteers needed," the man answered. "The hospital is looking for volunteers. I'm a volunteer."

"You're a volunteer?"

"Yeah. Gets me out of the house a few times a week. I talk to people, help people, and have a few laughs. I come here, do the best I can, and go home," said the man, flashing a thumb's up.

Ken nodded. The volunteer's words had struck a chord with him.

"Are there any volunteer positions open now?"

"Why, you're too young to volunteer here," the man said with a smile.

"Sixty-six."

"You're sixty-six? You don't look it. You look fresh out of the Marines. Here, let me check the list."

The gentleman opened the top drawer to his right, pulled out a folder and opened it. He ran his right index finger down the list.

"Bad news, young-timer. There's nothing here."

"Oh."

"Hold on. Let me check one other thing."

The gentleman picked up the phone and tapped four numbers.

"Hi, Maria? It's Rocket Man. Are you still looking for a volunteer there?" the gentleman asked. "Yeah? OK. Adios, mi amore."

Ken raised his eyebrows as the man hung up the phone.

"I thought so. Found something for you, Amigo. The emergency room needs somebody. Follow the red signs and ask for Maria. She'll take care of you."

"Emergency room?"

"Yeah, they've needed someone for a long while."

"Emergency room."

"Tough gig, but something tells me you can handle it."

"OK, thanks."

"No problem, partner. Maybe we can get a coffee sometime."

"Sure thing ... "

"Rocket Man," the man said, sticking out his hand.

"OK, Rocket Man. Ken. Nice meeting you."

"Nice meeting you, Kenny. Follow the red signs. And if you see the Grim Reaper, tell him I'm *not* here."

Ken smirked as he walked down the hall away from the desk. The bounce in his step continued.

"Emergency room. Emergency room. OK, emergency room," said Ken, pointing toward the small red sign on the tan wall.

Turning right, his footsteps echoed as he walked down an abnormally long hall. The right side was a wall and the left side was glass, through which he could see outside. The sun tried to peek from behind the clouds, shining through the leafless trees.

Ken stepped into a large lobby, filled equally with seats and expressionless people. Most of the patrons were on their cell phones. Some people tried to sleep, and no one smiled. The good vibes he had experienced not too long ago vanished. He cautiously walked toward the front desk in the back left corner.

"Maria?"

"Hiiiiii," the middle-aged, slightly overweight black hostess replied. "You the man who say he'd volunteer?"

"Well, I never said I'd … "

"We really need someone, Mista. We've never had no volunteer in here."

"What do you need someone to do?"

"Try to take people's minds off things. Other parts of the hospital, they OK. But here, don't nobody want to be in here, Honey."

"OK. How?"

"Just talk to people, Honey. Start a conversation and take their mind off what reason they in here for."

"Talk to people?"

"Yeah, just talk. We don't need you to be no doctor. We have doctors, but we don't have nobody to talk to people out here. You seem like a nice man. Just talk."

"Talk."

"Yeah, Honey. Talk."

"When do you need me to come in, if I want to do this?"

"Monday mornings, eight to noon. Everybody comes in Monday mornings. We always crowded Monday mornings."

"Just Monday morning?"

"Yeah, Honey. That's when we crazy busy in here, that and Saturday night, but, Honey, you don't want to be in here Saturday night. It's real crazy then. Like, *crazy* crazy."

"Do I need to apply or fill out a form or anything?"

"Honey, you the first person who has offered to come in here, and you a volunteer. We don't need no form. Just show up Monday morning at eight."

"OK, eight it is, Maria."

"And Mista, one piece of advice - don't wear no nice clothes."

"How come?"

"Oh, Mista, you find out."

Chapter 8

Beep-beep-beep.

Ken stretched his arm out from underneath the covers and hit the top of his digital alarm clock, the red numbers displaying 5:15. A big gulp of water; pajamas off; work-out gear on. Ken made his way to the basement, rode his stationary bike, showered, grabbed an apple and banana for the ride, and arrived at the hospital at 7:45 a.m. He saw Maria pull into the lot and park one row over. Ken scooted to her car, gave a friendly wave, and opened her door.

"See, you nice. I knew you was nice," said Maria, grabbing her brown, unzipped pocketbook.

They walked to the entrance for the emergency room, the sliding glass double doors humming as they opened. Ken looked to his right toward the lobby.

"It's not that busy."

"Give it thirty minutes, Honey. This place be packed."

Ken scanned the lobby from the front desk.

"Who should I talk to?"

"Just use your judgment, Honey. You seem like a smart man."

Ken cocked his head to the right before leaving the comfort zone of the front desk. He searched the room as he walked.

"No, no, no, no," he thought as he looked at the various people while he walked through the room's lobby area, turning to the right and stopping where the long hallway met the lobby. He stood and leaned against the wall, turning to see three groups of two people suddenly at the front desk. He looked through the glass and saw more people outside, making their way toward the entrance.

"Maybe I just got a non-talkative batch of people here," he thought as his eyes pinged from one person to another. "I'll let all these people sit down and I'll talk to them."

Four hours passed. Maria dealt with incoming patients nearly the entire time, and exhausted-looking people came and went from the waiting room. A few were alone, and those were the people who slept. Most of the would-be patients had someone with them. Ken made his way to Maria at noon.

"Hi."

"Hi, Honey."

"I didn't talk to anyone."

"I know. It's OK. You just nervous."

"I don't think I was nervous. I just think no one wanted to talk to me."

"You do better next Monday."

"Do you want me to come back? I feel I'm in the way; not doing anything."

"You ain't in the way. You come back next Monday. OK, Honey?"

"OK, Maria. I'll be in next Monday."

"And remember, don't wear no nice clothes."

"Yeah, you said that the other day. How come?"

"Honey, you find out."

Chapter 9

A week later, Ken turned off his car in the hospital parking lot at 7:45, and saw Maria pass through the gate when he closed his door. Again, he walked to her car and opened her door.

"Hey, Ken. I'm glad you here. I wasn't sure if you were going to come back."

"Yeah. I think I had first-day jitters last week. I'll dive right in today."

The pair walked through the door, and Ken immediately veered to the right toward the lobby. He spotted a middle-aged man with salt and pepper hair combed to the left sitting with a preschool-aged boy. The dad was on his cell phone.

"Hi. How are you today?" Ken asked the boy.

"Hi," said the dad, putting the cell phone in his pocket as he looked up. "He has a really bad fever. It's around 104 degrees. He's burning up, Doc."

"Oh, I'm not a doctor."

The man frowned.

"Can you get us a doctor? We've been here for two hours."

"Oh, ahh, no, I can't do that."

"Then what do you want?

"Ahh, to make you feel better."

"Do you have any medicine? The Motrin isn't touching this fever."

"Um, no, I don't have any medicine."

"Then what are you doing?"

"I'm just trying to help."

"Well, you don't have anything to help us, so if you don't mind ... "

"Sorry," Ken finished, walking back to the spot where he stood for four hours the previous week. The enthusiasm he had built up all week quickly evaporated.

Between patients, Maria waved Ken to come to the front desk. He quickly strode across the waiting room.

"Yes, Maria?"

"Good try, Ken."

"They didn't want to talk."

"Keep trying. You a nice man. People like you."

Ken turned toward the double door, feeling the cold air come through as it opened. He spotted an older, disheveled man walking toward the desk. Ken backed up to clear the way as the man stumbled in his direction. Ken quickly jerked his head away as the man, unshaven and wearing layers and layers of old clothes, walked in front of him. The stench was nearly unbearable.

Wanting to give the man his privacy, Ken swiftly walked and sat down in the lobby, which had already gained some patients in the short time he had been at the hospital. The man, walking unevenly and with a tilt to his left, fell into a seat. Ken tried to make eye contact, but the man's head was fully down. He had so much hair, Ken couldn't determine whether the man's eyes were open or not.

Ken waited, but the man still hadn't moved. Unsure, he decided the man couldn't have fallen asleep that quickly, and that he was alone. Pushing himself up, Ken walked to an open chair next to the man and gently placed himself in the seat to his left. The man remained motionless. Ignoring the atrocious odor, Ken searched for words.

"Hi?" Ken wondered. "Excuse me? How are you? What should I say?"

Ken opened and closed his right hand before wiggling his fingers. He lifted his hand and reached diagonally to his right, tapping the man twice on his left knee.

Instantly, in one motion, the man's head and shoulders lurched to the left.

SPLAT!!!

Vomit spewed from the man's mouth. A brown liquid, filled with worm-like figures, covered Ken's hand and right leg. Ken curled his nose and craned his head as far to the left as possible, the vomit trickling down to his right sneaker. He slowly stood, stepping to his left to avoid the man's innards, which now covered the floor in front of Ken. The vomit dripped off of Ken's hand as he walked to the front desk.

"Bathroom?" Ken asked Maria.

"Through these doors and straight ahead. It will be on your right."

Nodding, Ken made his way to the right of the desk for the metal double doors.

"I hope those aren't your nice clothes," Maria said.

"Not anymore."

Ken walked down the hall, past helpless patients on gurneys and nurses attentively working at various stations. He locked the door to the single bathroom and grabbed a handful of paper towels, wiping the throw-up off his right hand and sleeve into the toilet. After tearing off another batch of towels, Ken sat himself on the toilet seat, doing his best to rub off what he could. He shook his head as he felt wetness on his leg.

"Didn't see that coming."

Knock-knock-knock.

"Almost done in there?"

Ken turned toward the door. He slowly stood, threw the paper towels in the trashcan and turned the knob, pushing the door open. The father-son duo Ken had seen in the waiting room walked by him, into the bathroom, and closed the door.

Shaking his head and smelling like a sewer, Ken made his way down the hall, keeping his head down as he walked by the patients and the bustling nurses before exiting.

"I think I'm going to go home, Maria. I don't smell too good."

"OK, Ken. See you next week."

"Yeah, I'm not sure, Maria. I don't know if this is working out."

"It will work out. We like having you here, Ken. You a nice man."

Ken nodded and gave a small wave as he walked outside. The rush of the cold air prompted him to close his eyes.

Chapter 10

"Hi, Daddy."

"Nice to hear your voice, Sweetie. How's my big girl? Walking?"

"Almost. Cruising."

"Cruising?"

"Yeah, Daddy. That's when they walk while hanging onto something."

"Oh, yeah. That's right. That's great, Sweetie. Everything good with you?"

"Fine here, Daddy. Just busy. Teaching English 101 to 300 college freshmen, well, there's never a dull moment."

"Yeah, I can imagine."

"How are you, Daddy? Are you staying busy?"

"Oh, I'm always busy. I keep myself moving."

"Do you like your volunteer work at the hospital? It sounds interesting. You must meet so many people."

"Yeah, I don't think I'm going to do that anymore."

"Oh, no, Daddy. How come?"

"I don't do anything."

"You're helping people."

"I haven't helped anyone in the two weeks I've been there, and some guy threw up on me last week. I'm supposed to go in tomorrow, but I don't think I'm going to go back."

"Give it another chance, Daddy. You've only been twice."

"Yeah, I know."

"Give it more time. At least one more week."

"I don't know."

"One more week, Daddy. Please? I think you'll like it."

"We'll see. I'll sleep on it."

Chapter 11

Beep-beep-beep.

Ken reached back and pushed the button on top of his alarm clock. The time read the same as the previous two Mondays – 5:15 a.m.

"Last try, right here. If I don't help someone today, I'm going to tell them to find someone else."

Stationary bike, shower, and in the car by 7:15. Ken hesitated before putting the key in the ignition.

"Hold on," he said to himself as he opened the car door.

Ken opened the front door and turned to his left, opening a drawer at the end of the kitchen counter. Pens, pencils, tacks, paperclips and business cards filled the rectangular space. He reached in back, clutched his right hand and pulled it out. He looked at the Uno cards wrapped in a rubber band.

"Let's try this."

Ken stuck the cards in his coat pocket, got into his car, and drove to the hospital. When he arrived, Maria was already walking through the entrance.

"Hi, Ken. I thought maybe you weren't coming when I didn't have anyone to open my door today."

"I'll give it one more shot, Maria."

"Thanks, Ken. You a nice man."

Ken nodded and walked to the bustling waiting room, which was already full. He sat down in the one available seat; a chair attached to a table with a chair on the other side.

The lobby was particularly active, with patients being called into the emergency area and replaced by people who had just checked-in with Maria. Ken's watch read 11:57. He hadn't talked to anyone all morning, nor had he moved. Nobody seemed in need of help.

"Please, Mom?"

Ken looked to his right, where a thirty-something mother herded three young boys and carried another toward the chairs.

With all of the seats taken, the family sat on the floor, their backs to the windows.

"Please, Mom, can I have two dollars? I want M&M's," the tallest of the boys said.

The mother remained silent, cradling the youngest with her left arm while opening her over-sized tote bag with her right hand. The tallest child tugged on his mother's long down jacket, while the two other boys licked designs on the window.

Ken stood and walked toward the family, confident he could help the family in some capacity.

"Mom, pleaaaaaase," said the oldest, continuing to clutch his mom's jacket.

"Hi," said Ken, somewhat hovering over the family.

The mom glanced up, and the kids didn't react.

"Yes?" asked the mom, popping a piece of gum while she replied.

"Would you like a hand?"

"Excuse me?"

"Would you like a hand ... with your kids?"

"Would I like a hand with my kids?" said the mom, taken aback.

"Pleaaaaaaase, Mom. Pleaaaaaaaaase."

"Yeah. I'd like to help."

"Does it look like I need help?" the mom snapped.

Ken didn't reply, detecting the tone in her voice that indicated his help was unwanted.

"I don't *need* any help."

Taking a step back, Ken looked at his watch: it was 12:01. Shrugging his shoulders and letting out a sigh, he walked toward the front desk. He made eye contact with Maria between patients.

"Bye, Ken. See you next week?"

Ken stopped, shook his head, looked down, and turned toward the exit. Before he could move, the double doors opened, and the cold air hit him again. He closed his eyes and looked away, the chill penetrating his bones.

Opening his eyes, he saw a college-aged woman walk inside. She held her right forearm close to her side, and she carried a backpack and a teal plastic container in her left hand. Even though she moved slowly, the plastic carrier bounced as she walked.

Ken took a few swift steps toward the five-foot-seven-inch, freckle-faced girl, her brown hair pulled back in a ponytail.

"Can I help you?" asked Ken, his eyebrows raised.

"Thanks!" the upbeat girl said.

Ken reached and grabbed the yellow handle of the plastic box.

"Meow."

"Freddie, shhhh. It will be OK."

Ken lifted the bin eye-high. A cat balanced itself inside despite the movement.

"That's Freddie. He hates hospitals. Well, he's never been to a hospital, but he hates the vet. He probably thinks he's at the vet. You should hear him when he gets a shot. Woah, doggie, look out. Louder than a pack of seagulls on a piece of pizza at the beach."

Ken grinned as he listened.

"I hate leaving him alone. I take him everyplace. I can usually get around with him without any problem, but the strap on my backpack broke over the weekend."

Nodding, Ken didn't take his eyes off the young lady. He was struck by her spunk.

"Can I help you?" Maria asked.

"Hi. I'm back. Rhaymi Summers. I hurt my wrist again. I'm such a klutz," she said, turning and smiling at Ken, who replied with a small smile and a nod of acknowledgement.

"Is there a cat in there?" Maria questioned. "I'm not supposed to allow no pets in here. First it's cats, then dogs, and before you know it we have a whole zoo in here."

Rhaymi looked at Freddie in his carrier before turning to Ken, whose eyes bounced up and down between the top of the container and the girl's desperate eyes.

"Maria, this is ahh, Rhaymi. She's a friend of mine. She's a little stuck here. I'll watch the cat; I'll watch F-F-Freddie and make sure nothing happens. And, ahh, I look forward to seeing you next week when I come back to volunteer. OK? I'll bring you, ahh, cider; I'll bring you warm apple cider."

Maria looked at the carrier, which Ken was holding anxiously.

"I don't want no zoo, Ken."

"Nope, there won't be a zoo. I'm on top of it. I've got it."

"OK. Here, fill out this form," Maria smiled, handing Rhaymi a clipboard over the counter.

"Here," said Ken, grabbing the heavy backpack with his free hand.

"Oh, thanks," Rhaymi smiled.

"Ken, you such a nice man," Maria added.

"Ken?" asked Rhaymi as they walked toward the chairs. "You don't look like a Ken."

"What do I look like?"

"A Freddie."

"Freddie? Your cat's name is Freddie."

"Yeah, I know. Everybody looks like a Freddie to me."

Ken smiled as they continued to walk toward the waiting room, the cat carrier in one hand and the fluorescent green backpack in the other.

"Morgan?!" a nurse announced after she came through the metal double doors. "Faye Morgan?!"

A lanky, curly-haired, middle-aged woman stood and walked toward the nurse, freeing up the seat on the other side of the small table where Ken had been sitting minutes earlier.

"Perfect," said Ken, who slid Freddie and his carrier under the table. "Where would you like your backpack?"

Rhaymi grabbed the heavy bag with her left hand and plopped it on the floor in front of her, pushing it out with the soles of her sneakers before she placed her heels on top of it.

"Right here. Oh, God, that feels good. My feet are killing me. I think I need new sneakers. Do you think I need new sneakers? They're getting a little worn on the bottom."

"Yeah, if they're worn on the bottom you might need new sneakers."

"OK, I'll get new sneakers, right after my mid-terms."

"Mid-terms?"

"Yeah, I have my mid-terms coming up. I go to Pynchonton College. I'm in the nursing program."

"Nursing? Wow, that's impressive. You must be really smart."

Rhaymi snorted as she laughed and rolled her eyes.

"Hardly, Ken. I have to maintain an average no lower than a B-minus, and guess what I have? A B-minus."

"It must be hard. You have to know so many things; so many important things."

"Yeah, I'm constantly studying. Study, study, study. There's a lot to remember."

"Like the importance of paperwork?"

"What?"

"The importance of paperwork," repeated Ken, tapping the paper on the clipboard.

Another snort erupted from Rhaymi's nose.

"Ken!" she laughed, smacking her forehead with her left hand as her smile beamed. "I would have forgotten all about it. I'm such a dork."

Ken smiled before leaning down to look at Freddie, who remained silent. Rhaymi pulled the pen out from the top of the clipboard and placed it in her immobile right hand. She winced as she pulled her hand from her side.

"That's private, but if you want help, just ask," said Ken, concerned.

"Nope, I've got this. I've been through worse."

Rhaymi slid the clipboard up after every time she checked a box, twirling her feet in a circular motion as she did so.

"Do you want me to take the clipboard to the front desk for you?"

"Oh, Ken. You're the best."

Ken nodded, carefully grabbing the clipboard from Rhaymi and returning it to the front desk.

"See, Ken. You helpin'. You helpin'," Maria said.

A bright smile covered Ken's face as he walked back to the waiting area.

"Oh, I need to study; I need to study; I need to study," repeated Rhaymi as Ken sat down. "But I don't want to study; I don't want to study; I don't want to study. It's all becoming a blur. My brain is mush. I need a break."

Ken nodded, putting his hands in his coat pockets and leaning back. Without realizing it, his right hand was wrapped around something. He pulled it out, chest-high.

"Uno! I love Uno!" blurted Rhaymi, causing a few patients to lock in her direction.

"You like Uno?" Ken asked.

"Of course I like Uno. Everyone likes Uno. Who doesn't like Uno? Everyone in the world likes Uno. Well, maybe there are a couple communists who don't like Uno, but everyone else does."

"I see kids on their phones," Ken replied. "I don't see many kids playing Uno."

"Well, I love Uno; love it," said Rhaymi pointing directly at Ken. "I used to play by myself when I was a kid. Plus, I left my cell phone at my boyfriend's house."

"Um, do you want to play?"

"Do I want to play? Do I want to play Uno? Let's see, Ken, do I want to study or play Uno? Duh, Ken. What do you think? Deal those cards."

Stripping off the rubber band, Ken shifted in his seat and dealt the cards on the table. He looked over his hand, putting the colors together.

"Ken, you dealt six cards. It's supposed to be seven."

Surprised, Ken counted the cards in his hand out loud.

"One-two-three-four-five-six-seven."

"Ha! Made ya count, Ken. Made ya count."

Smiling, Ken dropped his head and started to laugh.

"Come on, Ken. That's the oldest one in the book. You've gotta be better than that."

"Yeah, well, get ready to lose at Uno."

"In your dreams, Old Man. I never lose at Uno. I'm the Uno Queen; Uno Queen of the World. I'm going to have that engraved on my headstone."

"Well, the Queen is about to be dethroned," announced Ken as he turned the top card over, revealing a Blue Two.

"You're a goner, Ken. Goner. Go write your will. See ya at the funeral."

Ken paused, recalling the two funerals he had attended in the last year. He shook off the unintended remark and pointed at his playing partner.

"You're up."

Rhaymi put down her first card. They exchanged turns, getting down to two cards each. Rhaymi couldn't play what was in her hand, drawing from the pile before looking up.

"Your turn," she said.

"You didn't put a card down," Ken replied.

"Yeah, I can't play. It's your turn."

"So keep drawing."

"What?" Rhaymi questioned.

"You draw until you can play. That's the rule."

"No, that's not the rule. You just draw once."

"House rules."

"House rules? We aren't at your house."

"We aren't at your house either. My deck. My rules. Draw, Missy pants."

"You suck, Ken. You really suck."

Ken smiled. Rhaymi drew a card, and again she couldn't play.

"Keep going."

"You suck, Ken," Rhaymi answered, taking another card before rolling her eyes.

"Keep that train going."

"I hate you, Ken."

"Rhaymi Summers?!"

The card-playing pair turned toward the loud request, seeing a nurse standing outside the metal double doors.

"Yes! Saved by the bell," said Rhaymi, tilting her head back.

"That was fast. You must know somebody."

"Yeah, I'm pretty popular."

Ken sprang from his seat and grabbed the bright backpack, picking it up and handing it to Rhaymi. He leaned down and began to slide the cat carrier out from under the table.

"Summers!!!" the nurse exploded, freezing Ken and Rhaymi, who raised her hand in acknowledgment. "Let's go!"

"I don't think you're getting Freddie in there," Ken whispered.

"I think you're right."

"Too cold to put him in the car."

"I think you're right."

"Here, I'll stay in the waiting area with Freddie. You go do what you have to do."

"Really?

"Yeah, it's OK. I'm a volunteer here. It's what I do. I help people."

"Wow, Ken, that's so nice of you. Thanks."

The broad-shouldered nurse aggressively waved Rhaymi in her direction.

"No problem. Here, leave your bag, too. I'll watch it."

Rhaymi stood still for a moment and smiled before moving toward the nurse, waving at Ken with her left hand as she walked through the metal door.

Chapter 12

Ken pulled back the top of his left sleeve an inch and twisted his wrist.

"Almost seven," he said peeking at the door, which he had done nearly every minute for hours.

The lobby in the emergency room had greatly quieted since the late morning and early afternoon. Maria departed three hours earlier.

"Shouldn't be much longer, Freddie," said Ken, wondering when the all-black cat last went to the bathroom or ate.

"Where's my Freddie, Freddie, Freddie, Freddie, Freddie," came a high-pitched voice from down the long hallway along the windows.

Ken turned to see Rhaymi burst into the room, her right wrist in a soft brace. She picked up the carrier and placed it on her lap as she rotated into the chair, her tiptoes pushing Freddie closer to her face.

"You OK?" Ken asked.

"Yeah, just a sprained wrist. No biggie."

"Seven hours for a sprained wrist?"

"I know, right?" Rhaymi quickly replied, shaking her head.

"They were so backed up. I should have brought my backpack. I could have gotten a lot of studying done."

"Oh, I'm sorry."

"Ken," Rhaymi answered, playfully slapping Ken on the left shoulder. "You didn't know. You were just trying to help. You did help."

Rhaymi leaned toward Ken and put her hands up to the sides of her mouth.

"There was no way I was getting Freddie past that prison guard of a nurse," she whispered. "If her relatives were in World War I, I'm pretty sure they were on the wrong side."

Rhaymi gave an exaggerated wink of her left eye at Ken, who smiled and shook his head.

"Yeah, you might be right. OK, well, it's been a full day. I'm going to head home now."

Ken stood, sticking out his chest and stretching his back.

"Do want me to walk you to your car?" Ken asked.

"I don't have a car here."

"You don't have a car here?"

"Nope, it's at school."

"At school? Well, how did you get here?"

"My boyfriend dropped me off."

"Oh, OK. How are you getting home?"

"My boyfriend will pick me up."

"OK. Is he on his way?"

"No, I haven't called him yet."

"Oh, that's right, you left your phone at his house."

"Yeah. What an idiot I am."

"Here, you can use mine," said Ken, reaching into his left pocket.

"Oh, wow. Thanks, Ken. I'll only be a second."

"Yeah, take your time. No rush."

Rhaymi inspected the flip phone in her left hand, rolling her wrist.

"What is this? Is this a prop from Star Trek? Beam me up, Scottie," she said, flipping open the phone and putting it up to her mouth. "Dude, this thing is old. I thought *you* were old, but geez."

"It's not that old. I've only had it two years."

"Not old? This thing's an antique. They had these in silent movies Does it even work?"

"It works."

"Well, beggars can't be choosers, I guess. I'll give it a whirl, Kenny Boy."

Rhaymi pushed the buttons and walked back toward the hallway along the window, stopping and looking outside at the dusk as she left the lobby area. Her hand flailed into the air once before she stepped fully into the hallway and out of Ken's sight. A minute passed, and then another. Ken's stomach growled. He hadn't eaten since before arriving at the hospital eleven hours earlier.

Rhaymi bounced back into the room, her hand and Ken's phone already reaching forward.

"Thaaaaank yooooou."

"You're welcome. Are you getting picked up?"

"Yup, he'll be here in fifteen minutes."

"Oh, fifteen minutes; that's not bad."

"What are you people doing here?!"

Ken turned toward the noise. A man staggered toward the front desk from the sliding double doors before turning right toward the lobby. It was the man who threw up on Ken a week earlier.

"Uh-oh," Ken said. "This isn't good."

"What are you people doing here?!" he repeated in the same tone, looking at the people in the waiting area.

Two security guards quickly jogged toward the drunk and nudged him in the opposite direction of the lobby.

"Do you know him?" Rhaymi asked.

"In a sense. He threw up on me last week. I was *helping* him," said Ken, using air quotes.

"That is so gross. I would have died right there. I mean, died right there on the spot."

"Yeah, it was bad. I stunk. I washed my clothes three times."

Rhaymi squished her face and pinched her shoulders together.

"Here, I don't want you by yourself while he's around. I'll stay until your boyfriend gets here."

"Ken, you're so sweet, but you don't have to do that."

"No, that's OK. Dad instincts. I can't leave you alone here with him around."

"I bet you're a great dad."

Ken shrugged his shoulders.

"What do you mean ... ?" asked Rhaymi, answering with her own shoulder shrug.

"Who am I to say? It's really up to my daughter to decide whether I'm a good dad or not, not me."

"You have a daughter?"

"Yup, and a granddaughter."

"You have a granddaughter? I don't believe that. You're not old enough to be a grandfather. I mean, you're old, but not that old. Not *old* old."

"She's six months old. I'm sixty-six; retired a few weeks ago."

"Retired? OK, I was wrong, you are old, Ken. Tough break."

Ken smiled again and shook his head, dropping it before looking up at Rhaymi.

"You're a good kid. You'll be a good nurse. You have good energy and know how to interact with people."

"My boyfriend thinks I'm crazy."

"Yeah, your boyfriend. When is he going to be here?"

"Fifteen minutes."

"OK, I guess I won't starve to death if I wait another fifteen minutes."

"We could go to the cafeteria," Rhaymi continued. "They have a great cafeteria here. Yeah, let's go. I should buy you dinner, Ken. You've been here a long time."

"No, no. Let's stay right here. I don't want your boyfriend to wait."

Ken and Rhaymi sat in the chairs in the lobby and continued to talk. Fifteen minutes passed, and then thirty, and then forty-five, and then an hour.

"You gave him the right hospital, right? Pynchonton?" Ken asked.

"Yeah, he dropped me off this morning. He loses track of time sometimes. I'm sure he'll be here any minute."

"It's been an hour."

Ken looked at his watch as Rhaymi nodded.

"I'd drive you to your dorm, but you really don't know me, and you shouldn't get in cars with strange men."

"You aren't strange, Ken. Well, maybe a little," said Rhaymi, giving Ken a punch on the left shoulder.

"Do you want me to drive you to your dorm? I could have you there in ten minutes."

"No, that's OK. I'm sure he'll be here any minute."

Ken nodded and tapped his fingertips together.

"Freddie has an iron bladder," added Ken, bending down to look at the cat through the holes in the carrier. "I don't know how he does it. He's so little."

"I know, right? He's a great cat."

"Well, I do not have an iron bladder. Excuse me. Freddie, I want to know your secret," Ken said as he stood.

The lady at the front desk pushed the button to open the metal double door after Ken flashed his volunteer badge. He walked quickly down the hall, keeping his eyes straight ahead and avoiding contact with patients. After going to the bathroom he washed his hands and walked down the hall, pushing a red button on the inside before reentering the lobby.

As the metal double doors opened he saw Rhaymi outside, opening the door to a white sports car. She placed the backpack on the floor and carefully lowered the cat carrier onto her lap before closing the door, reaching over with her left hand because her right hand was in the soft black cast. The car – a Corvette – quickly pulled away from the entrance and disappeared into the darkness.

Chapter 11

Apple cider in hand, Ken walked into the hospital at 7:40, eager to volunteer again following his positive experience the previous week. He placed the beverage in front of Maria's seat at the front desk and waited for her to arrive. A few minutes later, Ken greeted her with a big wave and smile as she walked through the sliding glass double doors. The blast of cold air didn't even affect his mood.

"Hey, Ken. Nice to see you back. And you brought me cider just like you said. You so nice, Ken. You so nice."

Ken stood with a smile, his hands in his pockets and his chest out as Maria sipped her cider. He wrapped his right hand around the Uno cards, eager to break the ice with someone again The double doors opened, and the coldness took another shot at Ken. The belligerent drunk from the two previous weeks walked into the hospital, stumbling directly to the lobby before he sat down.

"If he throws up on me again, you're paying for my dry cleaning," Ken said to Maria, who smiled and tapped him on the wrist as she prepared her computer.

"What are you people doing here?!" the man asked. His tone was angrier than it was the previous week, and this time he stumbled to the center of the half-full lobby.

Ken turned to look behind him, searching for one of the security guards. Maria stood and did the same, her face displaying a look of concern when she saw that no security guards were present.

"I've got it," said Ken, gently placing his left hand on Maria's shoulder before he walked toward the lobby.

"What are you people doing here?!" growled the man.

Jogging to the lobby, Ken put his palms up in front of his chest as he positioned himself in front of the drunk.

"Sir, how about we have a seat right here," Ken said gently, gesturing toward an open chair as he placed his left hand on the man's shoulders. The visitor thrust his left hand out of his pocket toward Ken, who felt something brush his left cheek. The man's momentum caused him to fall into the chairs. Ken took a step back. A pair of middle-aged security guards charged into the waiting room area, grabbed the man and pressed him to the floor

"What are you people doing here?!" the man gasped, the weight of two well-built men rendering him immobile.

A guard, whose flattop haircut fit his profession, pinned the man's left hand to the tile.

Ping.

Ken looked toward the faint noise. As the guards picked up the man, he saw a little pocketknife on the floor. It was open, the rusty blade no more than two inches long.

"Ken, are you OK?"

Maria stood in front of Ken, whose quickened heart rate began to subside.

"Yeah, I'm fine."

"You're bleeding, Ken."

"I am?"

"On your face," said Maria, rubbing her index finger on her own cheek.

Ken lifted his hand and touched his left cheek. As he pulled his hand back, he saw blood on his fingertips.

"Come here, Ken."

Maria grabbed Ken by the arm above the elbow and led him to the metal double doors, hitting the button at the front desk to open the doors. She took a few steps into the hall.

"Karen? Karen, Ken got cut by Mr. Swanson. Mr. Swanson had a knife."

The nurse sprang from her chair, recognizing the volunteer from previous weeks.

"A knife?"

"Yeah. Ken got cut on his face."

"I think my volunteering days are over, Maria."

Maria reached up and placed her hand on Ken's left shoulder, her eyes telling him she understood.

Chapter 12

White liquid bubbled on Ken's cheek after Karen dabbed an alcohol-filled cotton ball on the three-inch cut.

"Does it hurt?" Karen asked.

"It's OK," he replied.

Ken sat in a black plastic chair in a room one notch bigger than a closet.

"You're lucky."

"Oh, I know. I didn't see it coming. For a drunk, he moved fast."

Karen applied some ointment before pressing three medium-sized Band-Aids onto Ken's cheek, covering the cut.

"I'll be right back," she said, standing and leaving the room

Ken tapped the bandages with his fingertips. He stood and examined himself in the mirror on the wall, shaking his head.

"Not worth it."

The door opened, and Karen walked through carrying a needle, attracting Ken's gaze.

"Sorry. Your cut isn't deep, but we don't want to take any chances," she said.

Ken nodded, rolling his eyes and dropping his head.

"Can you take your coat off and roll up your sleeve, please?"

Unzipping his coat and sighing, he hung it on the hook on the back of the door before curling the right sleeve of his flannel shirt above the elbow. Ken didn't budge when Karen inserted the needle. He watching the ten-second procedure.

"You're all set, Ken. Sorry."

"It's OK. I think I'll just go home now, after I go to the bathroom."

Karen nodded as she left the room and Ken began to dress. He twisted the knob and turned to his right. He saw the two security guards standing outside the bathroom.

"Is that guy in there?" Ken asked as he neared the men.

Both nodded, not changing their facial expressions. Ken shook his head.

"I really don't want to see him. Is there another bathroom around here?"

"Go down this hall, take a right, and then straight ahead," the man with the buzz cut said with no expression.

"Thanks."

Ken followed the guard's instructions, entering into a part of the hospital he hadn't been in before. He read all of the labels on each door, remaining silent as he walked by nurse after nurse. No bathroom. He reached two oversized metal doors. He wasn't sure if those doors meant for him to not enter, or if they were for fire prevention safety.

Spurred on by the urgent pressure from his full bladder, Ken pushed through the doors. He stopped as they closed, and he recognized immediately how different he felt. He could see a nurse station far down the hall, but the hustle and bustle he felt in other parts of the hospital didn't exist here. He walked cautiously and was careful not to look into any rooms.

"Finally," he gasped, turning right and entering a one-person bathroom.

Taking his time, he washed his hands and dried them off. Uncharacteristically, he looked at his phone. No messages. He looked in the mirror.

"All right. Let's head home."

Exiting the bathroom, Ken looked in both directions, unsure which way to go. He took a few steps to his right before stopping, deciding he could probably find his way out if he went in the direction he came. He took a step before he stopped. He lifted his right ear higher, hearing a sound he couldn't quite decipher. He looked at the nurses' station, where they either didn't hear the noise or weren't concerned.

Deliberately taking a step, he stuck his head forward in an attempt to recognize the sound.

"What is that?" he thought. He took another step, and then another.

"Crying?" he wondered.

Noticing an open door, Ken moved as silently as possible toward the growing noise. He looked inside the unlit room, first seeing the television attached to the wall, and then the foot of the bed. He stopped, leaning his upper body to the right, where he saw a person sitting up in bed crying uncontrollably.

Ken's facial expression changed from curiosity to concerned. His eyes widened and his eyebrows jumped.

"Rhaymi?"

The girl looked toward the hallway and nodded. Ken turned to his right, slipping into the room before any of the nurses saw him.

"Rhaymi, what happened? Are you hurt?"

She shook her head, her ponytail flopping side-to-side in opposite directions. Her forehead housed a bandage, larger than the three Band-Aids on Ken's cheek. Rhaymi's volume came down a few levels, and her breathing improved. Ken stepped forward, grabbing the railing of her bed and leaning forward.

"Can I get you anything? Want me to get a nurse?"

Rhaymi shook her head a notch faster than before, a sign Ken took as to not ask any further questions.

"Sir, you aren't supposed to be in here. No guests allowed," a male voice said.

Ken turned and looked at the doorway, where a male nurse stood with his hands grasping the frame. Ken looked back at Rhaymi, who released a high-pitched whimper and squeezed her eyes closed.

"Um, I'm not a guest. Ahh, I'm a volunteer," he said, twisting his chest toward the doorway to display his volunteer badge.

Ken maintained his position as Rhaymi fought back her crying. The nurse left the doorway and walked in the direction of the station. Backing up two steps, Ken sat down in a chair, bending at the waist and placing his hands in his lap as he looked at the heartbroken girl.

After minutes of choking back her crying, Rhaymi took a big breath and exhaled. Ken's eyes softened, and a slight smile appeared on his face.

"There you go."

Rhaymi repeated her deep breathing, and then once more.

"Wow, that was bad," she said, wiping her nose straight up with her left palm. Ken shot up and stepped to his left, grabbing a box of tissues off of a small rolling table and handing it to Rhaymi.

"Thanks," she said, plucking two tissues out of the box before blowing her red nose. Ken nodded and smiled again, realizing Rhaymi was improving. She rolled up the tissues and shot them into the wastebasket near the door.

"Two points," she said with a chuckle.

"Nice shot."

"NBA, baby. Sign me up," she added, with a notch more energy.

Ken let out a little laugh, still uncertain of the situation.

"I should take up basketball. I'd be good at it. I'm fast, but I can't dunk. That basket is so high. It's, like, a mile high."

"Yeah, it's high."

"Really high."

"Have you ever played?" Ken asked.

"Yeah, in gym class a few times. I was good. I was so good no one could get the ball from me."

"I mean have you ever played on a team?"

"A team? Like a real team? Like a high school team?"

"Yeah."

"No, but my team in gym class always won. We never lost. I've never lost a basketball game."

Ken smirked and nodded, happy to hear the excitement return in Rhaymi's voice.

"Have you ever played basketball, Ken?"

"A little, when I was younger. You know, when I was a kid."

"They had basketball back then?"

"Easy," Ken said as Rhaymi smiled, leaning back in her bed.

"I could beat you in basketball, Ken. I'd run circles around you."

"Yeah, you probably could. Not my sport," he replied, sitting back and putting his hands into his coat pocket, where he felt the Uno cards with his right hand.

Ken looked down at his pocket, and then back up at Rhaymi with a devilish expression.

"But you can't beat me at this," he said, extending the cards in his right hand toward Rhaymi.

"Ken!" she said, smacking her hands on the mattress.

"You want to talk about a mile high? That handful of cards you had last time we played was a mile high; maybe two miles. You needed an oxygen tank just to take a card."

"Are you looking for a fight?" Rhaymi asked. "Are you looking to fight me, Ken?"

"I'm looking for someone to beat in Uno, and I just found her."

"You're toast, Ken; toast. Deal the cards, Old Man."

Ken turned to his left and wheeled the small table between his chair and the bed. He placed the cards on the table as he adjusted the height.

"Just deal, Ken."

"Take it easy, Missy pants."

Pulling the rubber band off and tapping the cards on the table, Ken dealt seven cards each.

"Ken?"

"What's the problem this time? Cards too slippery? Too heavy? Inside-out?

"Ken?"

"What?"

"Your new nickname is Irene."

"Huh?"

"Your new nickname is Irene."

"Why?"

Rhaymi slapped a card on the table, forcing it to shake. It was a Wild Draw Four.

"Draw Four! Good night, Irene!"

Ken turned his head as he laughed before taking four cards from the top of the pile.

"Pick a color, Irene."

"What?"

"Pick a color."

"You're supposed to pick the color. You had the Draw Four."

"Just pick a color."

"OK, mauve."

"Don't be a wise guy, Irene. Just pick a color."

"All right, all right. Red."

"You want red?"

"Yeah, red."

"OK, Irene."

Rhaymi slammed her next card on the table, forcing the cards to bounce out of place. The card was another Wild Draw Four.

"Goodnight, Irene," she shouted with her eyebrows raised. "Red means dead. Hahaaaaa."

Shaking his head again, Ken plucked four more cards from the deck.

"Who has the stack of cards now, Irene? Don't climb up on those cards and jump, Irene. You might hurt yourself."

Rhaymi smiled as she rocked back-and-forth while sitting up in her bed. Ken adjusted his cards, putting all of the colors together.

"You're so kind, Rhaymi. Your parents must be so proud of you," Ken said, leaning forward with a smile.

Rhaymi stopped rocking. Her face froze. She slowly pulled a card from her hand, placing a Green Draw Two on the table. Sensing a change in the room's atmosphere, Ken stayed silent as he took two cards. Rhaymi responded by putting another Green Draw Two face up. Ken reached to take two more cards.

"Sir, there are no guests allowed in this part of the hospital."

Ken shifted his hips so he could turn all the way to the right. A black lady with a touch of gray in her curly hair stood in the doorway.

"Hi. I'm not a guest. I volunteer in the waiting area for the emergency room," he answered with a concerned smile.

"OK, then you can go back to the waiting room. I need to talk to Rhaymi."

Ken looked at Rhaymi, whose face was expressionless as she looked at her bed sheets.

"Ahh, OK. Yup."

Standing and moving the table back into the corner, Ken grabbed the cards and the rubber band, sticking the items into his right pocket.

"Do you want me to wait for you in the waiting room?"

Rhaymi nodded slightly, her face maintaining her anxious look.

"OK, I'll wait for you."

Rhaymi again nodded, this time looking up at Ken.

The woman, wearing a white lab coat and giving off a presence of authority and professionalism, stepped aside as Ken walked through the door and down the hall. He took a few strides before seeing the male nurse standing at the station. Ken lifted his right hand and extended his index finger, getting the attention of the male nurse, walking quickly in his direction.

"Yeah?"

"What happened to Rhaymi?" Ken asked.

"You know her?"

"Yeah, I know her. She's a friend."

"She was in a car accident."

"Car accident?"

"Yeah, ran right into a tree, head on."

"A tree?"

"Yeah. Boom; head on. She's crazy."

Ken frowned and his head pulled back, puzzled by the remark from the male nurse.

"Well, lots of people get into accidents," Ken replied.

"Not on purpose."

"On purpose?"

"Yeah, on purpose."

"What do you mean, on purpose?"

"She drilled her car right into a tree on purpose. I saw the car on my way to work, over near the golf course in Heapstown."

"A tree?"

'Right into a tree, square on."

'People don't drive cars into trees on purpose."

'She did. That chick is nuts."

Ken looked down the hall toward Rhaymi's room and then back at the male nurse.

"Mister, you know where you are, right?"

"Pynchonton Hospital. I was born here; my kids were born here; my wife ... um. I volunteer here. I volunteer in the waiting area in the emergency room."

"Yeah, I know, you told me already. But do you know where you are right now, as in, right here where you're standing."

Ken looked at the floor and then back up at the male nurse, shaking his head.

"You're in the psych ward."

"Psych ward?" blurted Ken, drawing the attention of the three other nurses at the station.

"Dude."

"Sorry," answered Ken, raising his hands chest high. "So, why would a person be in here?"

"Lots of reasons. Sometimes they tried to hurt themselves, or had a breakdown, or maybe they were about to do something, well, crazy. And that girl you were talking to is crazy."

"She's really smart, and very outgoing. And funny, she's really funny."

"Buddy, none of that matters," said the male nurse as he waved off Ken. "She's crazy."

Ken rubbed his forehead with the back of his right hand, looking down the hall again. He saw the older lady leave Rhaymi's room and walk through the metal double doors in the hall, clipboard in hand. Ken's eyebrows raised and he tugged his chin before looking at the male nurse.

"I forgot my hat. I'll be right back," he said to the male nurse, jogging back to the room.

Ken looked at the closed metal doors before stepping into Rhaymi's room.

"Rhaymi, were you in a car accident?"

"Yeah. My boyfriend is going to kill me."

"What?"

"My boyfriend is going to kill me. It was his car."

"The Corvette?"

"Oh, my God, he would, like, *really* kill me if I crashed his Corvette. No, I crashed my car, the one he bought for me."

"Bought for you?"

"Yeah, he bought me a car last summer. He buys me lots of things."

"Uh-huh. So what happened?"

"A deer ran right in front of me. I swerved to miss it and hit the tree."

"Oh, well, yeah, a deer can be tough, especially in the morning."

"Oh, this didn't happen in the morning. It happened last night.'

'Last night? You've been here since last night?"

"Yeah."

"Well, you look OK other than the bandage on your head. Are you hurt?"

"No, I feel fine. I really want to leave because I have a mid-term tomorrow I need to study for."

"Oh, that's right, you have exams this week."

"Yeah, I *really* need to study."

"So how are you getting home?"

"My boyfriend will pick me up."

"Will he be on time this time?"

"Oh, yeah, he's really good to me. He was late last week because he forgot his wallet at home and had to go back to get it."

"Oh, OK, I guess that makes sense."

"Excuse me."

Startled, Ken turned around, seeing the lady in the lab coat in the doorway again.

"Sir?"

"Sorry, I forgot my hat in here," said Ken in a slightly higher pitch than his normal tone.

Ken moved the table, stuck his hands in his pockets, and tapped the outside of his jacket.

"I can't find it. I guess I left it in the waiting area for the emergency room, which is where I'm going now. See ya, Rhaymi."

"Bye, Irene."

Chapter 13

The cup filled with cider rested to the right of Maria's computer.

"Can I ask you a question, Maria?"

"Of course, Ken."

"What do you know about the psychiatric unit?"

"Oh, they have special people over there. It ain't easy working there. Never know what's gonna happen next."

"Yeah. So, who goes there?"

"Lots of folks. They usually come here first; then, after they get evaluated, they move over there."

"Who evaluates them?"

"A nurse or a doctor. And once they over there, a counselor will talk to them to determine what they need and how we can best help them."

"Right. Well, I guess that makes sense."

"There are lots of people with dark corners. You wouldn't believe all the people we send over there."

"Dark corners?"

"Yeah, dark corners – problems people don't want no one else to know. Lots of people with dark corners, Ken. Lots."

Ken felt a shot of cold air. He turned to see a young mother with a baby and a toddler walking toward the front desk.

"I guess I'll just go sit down," he said, stepping back so the family could check in at the front desk.

Pulling back the tip of his left sleeve, Ken saw that his watch read 9:01. He was done with volunteering, but he said he would wait for Rhaymi. He sat down, facing the windows on another gray morning.

"She's been here since last night and she isn't hurt. It shouldn't take that long," he thought, touching the Band-Aids on his cheek.

Ken checked his watch, and again, and again, and so on for the next five hours. He rubbed his eyes, slightly drained from the morning's events. He stood and walked toward the windows, bending over to touch his toes. Coming up, he stretched his hands to the ceiling and let out a long sigh.

Beep. Beep.

Ken stepped closer to the window and looked outside. He pressed his hands against the window.

Beeeeeeeeeeep.

Looking to his left, Ken saw a white Corvette. Rhaymi, in regular clothes, sprinted for the car and swung the door open, then quickly hopped in a moment before the car pulled away. Ken clearly saw Rhaymi in the front passenger seat as the car sped by the emergency room entrance, hooked left and exited the parking lot.

Frowning, Ken turned and walked toward the double doors, motioning to Maria to let him in. He marched past the nurses and patients, firmly pushing open the metal double doors to the psychiatric ward and continuing to walk with a purpose toward the station for the nurses. He briefly stopped at the room Rhaymi had occupied, only to see it empty. The male nurse stood in the center of the hall in front of the station.

"Excuse me, can you help me?" Ken asked, looking sternly at the gentleman. "Where did the girl go? Where's Rhaymi?"

"Dude, I told you, that girl is nuts. She was walking down the hall and when someone asked her where she was going, she just started running."

"Running? Why?"

"Why? You can't just leave a hospital whenever you want. There's a process. You gotta check out."

"Are you saying she just left?"

"Yeah. Just left. She's crazy."

"Excuse me."

Ken jumped forward and turned quickly as he felt a tap on his right shoulder.

"God!" he gasped.

"Sorry," said the same black lady Ken had seen going into Rhaymi's room in the morning. "You know Rhaymi, right?"

"Yeah," Ken replied after hesitating.

"Come with me, please."

Chapter 14

A mini palm tree stood in a dark brown flowerpot in the left corner of the nicely decorated office. Ken was struck by what he presumed was a family photograph, a stunning, smiling family. Three framed diplomas were designed in the shape of a triangle on the wall above the desk – Springfield College, Boston College, and Dartmouth College.

"Hello, I'm Dr. Harding. I'm a psychologist here at the hospital."

Dr. Harding extended her hand. Ken was impressed. The doctor had a presence about her – a certain quality that only comes with wisdom and experience.

"Hello, Doctor," he answered, shaking her hand. "Ken Roy."

"Thanks for agreeing to talk to me."

"Sure. No problem."

"Do you know Rhaymi?"

Ken briefly paused before answering, "Yeah, I know her."

"Do you know her well?"

"I've gotten to know her a little here recently. I know she's studying nursing at Pynchonton College. She's a sophomore."

"Anything else?"

"She seems very smart, and she's really good with people."

"She's a lovely girl."

Ken nodded and gave the doctor a half-smile, not sure where the conversation was going.

"Do you know she's been in here four times in the last two months?"

"Four times?"

The doctor opened a green folder on her desk.

"In February she was in with a wrist injury."

"No, that was last week. I was here when she came in. I was volunteering."

"No, Mr. Roy. That was the second time she came in for her wrist. The first was in February – slipped on some ice."

Ken nodded as the doctor looked down at her notes.

"Then a month ago she was in with alcohol poisoning. Had to have her stomach pumped; said she got a little carried away with some friends doing shots. Then she was back last week with another wrist injury, and yesterday it was the car accident – a dog ran in front of her."

"No, it was a deer."

"Well, our report says a dog, Mr. Roy."

Nodding, Ken's face grew concerned.

"Do you know anything about Rhaymi's personal life?"

"Um, I know she has a boyfriend, and, ahh, she's good at cards."

The doctor sat stone-faced, taking in the information.

"That's it, really. Seems like a nice girl."

"Anything else?"

"No. No, I don't think so."

"OK, Mr. Roy, I thank you for your time."

"Can I do anything to help?"

"Well, if you see Rhaymi and you see anything that's, I don't know, out of place, could you give me a call or send me an email?" the doctor asked, handing Ken a business card.

"I don't know if I'll ever see her again, but sure. Of course," he said, taking the card and tucking it into his worn black wallet.

"Great. Thank you, Mr. Roy."

"I'm sorry. I guess I don't understand. Why did you want to talk to me? Did Rhaymi do something wrong?"

"No, Mr. Roy, not at all."

"So I don't understand the problem."

"Well, I want to study the reports a little more, and all of that information is confidential anyway."

Ken nodded.

"But I'll ask you a question, Mr. Roy, because it's a question I'm sure you would have asked yourself at some point. How many nineteen year olds do you know who go to an emergency room four times in two months?"

Ken lifted his head stared at the wall.

"None."

"And I don't either, Mr. Roy. I don't either."

Chapter 15

Click.

Ken turned his car lights off and stepped onto the black pavement, closing the door to his 2008 Camry. He could see his breath, and he felt water coming from his eyes on the cool April morning. He arrived in Pynchonton Park earlier than his running friends, hoping to get in a five-kilometer loop before joining his mates. He was scheduled for eighteen miles – 18.6 to be exact. He hoped to run in the Milltown Marathon in three weeks, the flat 25.2-miler just twenty minutes from his house. It would be his thirty-third marathon, but his first in two years.

Six red Gatorades stood on a towel on top of his trunk, as well as a banana, cut in half. With a touch of his toes he was off, dressed in black running pants and a black running coat. The park was peaceful this time of morning, with no cars and few people.

Returning to his car after an uneventful first loop, Ken saw his friends.

"No one likes a showoff, Ken," joked Ivan Anders.

"Don't listen to him, Ken. He's just jealous," added Michael Crum.

Another friend, Russ Holt, grabbed one of the Gatorades and gave it a short toss toward Ken.

"How many laps today, Ken?" Russ asked.

"Six."

"Six? Still planning on doing Milltown?"

"That's the goal."

"Going for a time?"

"Nope. Just want to stay steady and finish."

"Oh, well, if you stay healthy today you should be fine."

Ken nodded as he chugged the Gatorade before putting it down on his trunk.

"Come on, girls. Let's go. I'm getting cold standing here," Ivan said.

"Yes, dear," Michael quipped.

Ken smirked as the four began their run together. The group started four abreast but, as always, they split into two groups of two, with the pairs changing at the start of every lap after they rehydrated with their drink of choice.

Ivan and Michael dropped out for after the group's third lap, and Russ stopped after the fourth.

"You good to do the last one on your own?" Russ asked.

"I'm getting a little tired, but I should be OK. It's just one more 5K. I can handle it."

"You here next week?"

"Yeah."

"Usual time or early again?"

"Usual. I came early today because of the eighteen."

"Don't sell yourself short, Ken – 18.6," Russ complimented.

"Right."

"OK, see you next Saturday. Bye, Ken."

"Bye, Russ."

Ken looked at his running watch. His breathing was good, which was an encouraging sign, but his legs became more and more tired the longer he ran. He focused to keep his stride normal, ignoring the increasing number of cars and people in the park. His watched beeped, as it did every mile. He lifted his left wrist and stuck his arm straight out to force the sleeve back a sliver. He looked at his watch, which read eighteen miles.

The toe of Ken's right sneaker hit something, propelling him forward. He lifted his left hand in front of his mouth a moment before he hit the ground, and his forehead was first to touch the cold, unforgiving pavement. His left hand pressed into his mouth, and then both knees thumped to the blacktop.

Dazed, Ken looked back toward his feet, noticing a speed bump he failed to see. He shook his head, disappointed in himself that he wasn't more careful. He pushed himself up onto all fours, staring at the road.

"Hey, mister, are you OK?" a female voice asked.

Craning his head to the right, Ken struggled to look up.

"Ken?!" shouted Rhaymi, as she crouched toward the fallen runner.

Ken's spirits lifted, although physically he could only manage a slight nod of the head.

"Ken," Rhaymi repeated, stretching her right hand toward his forehead. "You're bleeding."

Ken rolled over to sit down on the pavement. He reached up with his right hand and touched the left side of this forehead, seeing the blood as he pulled his hand away. Rhaymi yanked her sneaker off and then her white sock, pressing it against Ken's forehead.

"I know this is gross, Ken, but we have to stop the bleeding. We have to get you cleaned up."

Nodding, Ken slowly stood, making sure he had his balance before he walked forward.

"Where are we going?" Rhaymi asked.

"Back to my car," he answered, still holding the sock to his head. "It's just a half mile this way."

"You don't look good, Ken. That's a pretty good gash on your head, and you look a little pale."

"I just need a drink of Gatorade."

"You look like garbage; real crap."

"Thanks."

"I was getting ready to pass you, too. You're pretty slow, Ken."

"You really know how to cheer a guy up."

"How far were you going?"

"I just hit eighteen – literally."

"Eighteen?! Wow, that's awesome, Ken. Eighteen. OK, I take back what I said. That's really great. I ran thirteen last week. I'm going to run Boston next Monday."

"The Boston Marathon?"

"Yeah, Boston."

"Where did you get your bib number?"

"What's a bib number?"

"You know, a bib number ... the number you wear to show you're officially in the race."

"Oh, I don't have a number. I'm going to run as a brandit."

"Brandit?

"Yeah, a brandit."

"You mean bandit."

"Brandit. Bandit. Whatever. I'm going to go run Boston."

"Ahh, sorry to rain on your running parade, but I don't think so. Bandits aren't allowed anymore at Boston."

"Not allowed? My boyfriend's father ran as a bandit once when he was in college."

"Yeah, bandits were allowed, back in the day. But those days are gone. There's security all over the place, especially since the bombing year. No number; no race."

"No race? But I want to run a marathon. It's on my bucket list."

"A little young for a bucket list, aren't you?"

"I have a long bucket list, Ken. I need to get started when I'm young."

"How far is your long run? Thirteen?"

"Yeah, that's far. Not as far as eighteen, but still pretty far."

"That is far, but it's only half of a marathon."

"How far is a marathon?"

"You don't know how far a marathon is, and you were going to run Boston?"

Rhaymi nodded, ready for Ken's response.

"Every marathon is the same distances – 26.2 miles."

"Oh, wow, now that's far. Really far. Like, really, really far."

"Sure is."

"I don't know if I could do that."

"Well, you've done thirteen, which is pretty good, and you have young legs. If you were smart about it and caught a few breaks, you could finish, maybe."

"Do you think so?"

"Yeah, if you were smart. Conservative. How do you usually run?"

"With my arms."

"Don't be wise," Ken said as Rhaymi smiled. "What's your pace? Do you negative split your long runs?"

"Ken, I don't know what you're talking about. Negative pits. Hey, man, I just run. When I step out that door, I go, you know what I mean?"

"Yeah, I know what you mean, and if that's the case I don't think you'd make a marathon, Rhaymi, sorry. You just haven't put in the mileage, and you don't quite have the experience. I actually think you'd have a bad experience."

"Bad experience?"

"So, based on what you told me, my guess is you'd make it to fifteen or sixteen miles, get really tired really fast, and then walk the last eight miles or so.

"Walk eight miles?"

"Yeah, if you weren't hurt, or sick."

"Sick?"

"When you run a marathon, you need to refuel your body, like putting gas in a gas tank for a car. You need to drink and eat to keep you going."

"Eat and drink when you run? I've never done any of that."

The Gatorade bottles were lined along the trunk, with five empty bottles and one full as they returned to Ken's car. He grabbed the full drink and handed it to Rhaymi.

"Oh, no thanks. I'm good."

Ken nodded before chugging the entire bottle and placing it back on his trunk.

"Refueled."

"How many marathons have you run, Ken?"

"Thirty-two."

"Wow, you're, like, a marathon man – Ken the Marathon Man."

"Ha, yup. I've done Boston seven times, always with a number."

"So you don't think I could run at Boston."

"No chance. Security is too tight."

"Is there another one I could do, that I could still sign up for?"

"Um, yeah. There's one in Milltown in three weeks. I'm going."

"Oh, Ken, can I run with you?"

"You want to run with me?"

"Yeah. Sure. Why not?"

"Well, I don't *just run*," said Ken, leaning forward and flashing Rhaymi air quotes. "I run a very specific pace. I'm not fast and I'm not flashy, but I stay steady and get to the finish line."

"Sounds boring, just like you, Ken."

"Yeah, I guess it does."

"Ken, let me see your cut," said Rhaymi, grabbing the sock out of Ken's hand.

The bleeding slowed, but it didn't stop, and bits of dirt from the road were spread throughout the gash. Rhaymi plopped herself on the ground, flicked her other shoe off, and grabbed her sock.

"Here, you need to keep pressure on it. That's the best way to stop the bleeding."

Ken took the sock, looked at it, and applied it to his forehead.

"Ken, can you see?"

"Yeah, my eyesight is fine."

"No, I mean to drive."

Ken rotated his head, looking at different points ahead of him.

"Ahh, well, I can, but my hand is right in front of my left eye."

"Do you want to call an Uber?"

"What's an Uber?"

"What's an Uber!?" shouted Rhaymi, snapping forward and slapping Ken on the shoulder. "Man, Ken, you are so old."

"I'm pretty old."

"Yeah, you are."

Ken opened the door to the back passenger seat and put the bottles on the floor one at a time.

"Ken, should you drive?"

"Yeah, I don't know."

"Do you want me to drive you home?"

"Oh, you don't have to do that. I'm all right."

"Ken, really, you shouldn't drive, especially with a head injury. You feel OK now, but you don't know how you're going to feel in ten minutes. You could pass out."

Closing the back door to the car, Ken sighed.

"Ken, you shouldn't drive," continued Rhaymi, who squealed and made an explosion sound, thrusting her hands into the air. "Trust me, Ken, been there, done that."

"Yeah, but then your car is here. You don't want to leave your car in the park."

"My car's in a junkyard, Ken. I ran here; it's only a mile from my dorm."

Ken pulled the white sock away from his head, seeing a good amount of blood. He looked at Rhaymi.

"You aren't going to crash again, are you?"

"I don't know, but I know I can drive better than you right now, so take a chance and hop in."

Smiling, Ken got into the front seat of his car on the passenger side. Rhaymi bounced as she shot into the driver's seat and slammed the door.

"Buckle up, Old Man. Get ready for the ride of your life."

Chapter 16

Thump. Thump.

Ken and Rhaymi walked toward the front door of the house. The ride was uneventful as Rhaymi drove the speed limit at Ken's repeated requests. He stuck his hand toward his chauffeur at the base of the steps with his palm up. Rhaymi placed the keys into his hand before he wiggled them to find the right one.

Stepping inside, Ken planted the keys on the kitchen counter.

"Where's your alcohol, Ken?"

Perplexed, Ken turned toward Rhaymi.

"Rubbing alcohol, Ken. Not that kind of alcohol. I don't drink."

"You don't drink? Really?" remarked Ken, recalling his conversation with Dr. Harding.

"Nope."

"Oh, well, that's good."

"Rubbing alcohol, Ken. Need it."

"Hold on. I'll go get it," said Ken, who started to walk out of the kitchen.

"No. You just sit down. You have a head injury. No walking. Sit."

Ken nodded slightly and made his way toward the family room.

"Good, Ken. Later we'll work on stay and roll over."

Cracking a full smile for the first time since falling, Ken carefully sat in his recliner.

"Rubbing alcohol; cotton balls; Band-Aids. Dónde estás?"

"Closet in the bathroom upstairs, about eye level."

"Gracias, *Señor*," Rhaymi replied, sprinting out of the room.

Boom-boom-boom!

Ken heard Rhaymi sprint up the stairs and open a door. There was a pause before he heard the next sound.

Boom-boom-BOOOOOM!

Ken turned toward the noise that shook the house, and saw Rhaymi land at the bottom of the stairs carrying the medical supplies. Rhaymi ripped open the plastic bag for the cotton balls, sending a few onto the tan rug. She twisted the cap of the rubbing alcohol off and flipped the bottle upside-down after placing a cotton ball at the opening. She reached up and took the sock out of Ken's hand.

"OK, relax, Ken. This will only hurt a lot."

Shaking his head, Ken closed his eyes with a smile on his face. Rhaymi gently dabbed the cotton ball on Ken's forehead, taking a break every few seconds to apply more liquid. Ken could feel pieces of dirt drop onto his right cheek. Ken melted into the chair, feeling long, soft, horizontal strokes on his forehead.

"Almost done, Ken. I charge a hundred dollars an hour, by the way."

Ken opened his eyes and saw Rhaymi putting the cap back on the bottle. She placed her hands on the arms of the chair and leaned forward, gently blowing on Ken's forehead. Rhaymi's face was an inch from Ken's. He looked at her lips, and then her chin. Rhaymi's shirt brushed Ken's running jacket. Rhaymi pulled back and bent over, grabbing the box of Band-Aids. Ken stayed motionless, watching Rhaymi's movements.

Positioning her feet to the side of the chair, Rhaymi dropped her knees a few inches and applied a large bandage to the gash. Ken looked up at Rhaymi's hands.

"There you go, Ken. Good as new."

Ken rubbed his right hand in small circles on the bandage.

"Well, maybe not good as new. You look like you were in a fight .. and lost."

"Thanks, Kid."

"No problem, Old Man."

Rhaymi collected the cotton balls off the floor and walked into the kitchen. She found the trashcan under the sink on her own and returned to the family room.

"Hey, Ken. Who's that?" asked Rhaymi, pointing toward the wall above his chair. "Is that your daughter?"

Ken swiveled in his chair, looking up at the framed photograph of Brooke from high school. "Yeah, that's Brooke; her senior picture."

"She's hot."

"Yeah, she's a pretty girl."

"Is she home?"

"Nope, she's in Florida. She's a teacher at a college down there."

"Oh, that's right. And you have a granddaughter. Do you have a picture of her?"

"Yeah, upstairs."

"Man, you're a grandfather."

"Yup, I'm a grandfather."

"Geez, Ken. You're older than I thought. You're old. Like, *old* *old*."

"I keep walking into that one, don't I?"

"And who's this? Is this your wife? She's pretty."

Ken swiveled back around in his chair. Rhaymi was standing next to the coffee table in front of Ken's recliner, where Marie's head-and-shoulders picture sat in a frame.

"Yup, that's Mrs. Roy."

"I love her hair. Is she coming home soon?"

"Nope."

"Ken, don't be a poop. She looks so nice. Can I meet her?"

Ken gave her a small smile and looked at the picture.

"She passed away three months ago."

"Oh, Ken. I'm sorry," Rhaymi said, dropping her head. "Sorry I said anything. I'm such a blabber mouth."

"You didn't know. You asked a question – a harmless question. There's nothing wrong with that."

Rhaymi maintained her position - motionless and looking at the floor.

"Hey, Rhay. It's OK. You didn't know," said Ken, drawing a slight nod from Rhaymi. "Do you want to know how she passed away? You might find it interesting."

Rhaymi lifted her chin and looked at Ken, nodding.

"She had an aggressive form of ALS."

"Lou Gehrig's Disease? That's so interesting, and sad; really sad. ALS is the worst. I haven't studied that yet, but my neighbor died from that the day before I came here for college my freshman year. I couldn't go to the funeral because I couldn't cancel my flight."

"You're not from the area?"

"Nope. California."

"California?"

"Yeah, Malibu."

"What brought you all the way out here? You're a long way from home."

"I was looking for a nursing school in Massachusetts. I love all of the Boston teams; Sox, Pats, Bruins, Celtics – I love 'em all."

"Really?"

"Tom Brady is God, and how many World Series have the Sox won since 2004? Four?"

"Yeah, we're pretty spoiled here. I think Boston teams have won twelve championships since 2001. Good run."

"I know. It's awesome. I go to the Patriots all the time. My boyfriend has season tickets. He has a box; a box, Ken. How cool is that?"

"That is pretty cool, especially when the weather's bad."

"Yeah, bad weather sucks, although I don't mind running in the rain."

"So, speaking of running, do you want to run that marathon?" Ken asked.

Rhaymi sprang off the floor and grabbed Ken by his jacket, inches away from his face.

"Yes, Ken. Yes. I want to run. When is it? When is it?"

"Three weeks, in Milltown at eight in the morning."

"Three weeks. Cool."

"Do you have a car? If not, I can pick you up."

"No, that's OK. My boyfriend can bring me."

"Your boyfriend. OK; well, you need to be there at least by 7:30 so you can register, warm up, and get to the start."

"OK."

"You can't be late."

"OK."

"I'll wait for you at the registration table."

"KO."

"Come on, Rhay, I'm serious."

"I know, Ken. I know. Milltown Marathon at eight in the morning, meet at the registration table at 7:30. It's filed, Ken," Rhaymi said, tapping the left side of her head with her finger. "I'll be there."

Ken gave a thumbs up to Rhaymi, who replied with a double thumbs up and a wink. Recalling his conversation with Dr. Harding, Ken asked a calculated question.

"So, does your boyfriend go to college with you?"

"Oh, no. He has a job at Tatum Financial in Pynchonton. He's a financial planner."

"A financial planner? Really? Wow, that's impressive."

"Yeah, he makes a lot of money. He has his own house. It has a pool and a hot tub. The hot tub is sooooo nice. We go in it all the time."

"House? How old is he?"

"Twenty-four."

"Twenty-four? He has a house with a pool at twenty-four?"

"Yeah, it's really nice. It's on a dead end street right next to the golf course in Heapstown."

"I know that area. It's really nice over there; a lot of big homes."

"Yeah, he's a great boyfriend. I'm really lucky."

"Well, he sounds like a good guy."

"He is."

"So, we should get you back to your dorm. Thanks for patching me up."

"Ken, I don't think you should drive. You feel fine now, but you don't know how you're going to feel later."

"No, I'm good," he answered, standing. "See? No problems."

"No, you should relax today. You fell right on your noggin. That's a pretty good cut you have. I'll call my boyfriend to pick me up. Oh, shoot, I don't have my phone."

"Here, go in the kitchen, on the end of the counter there's a phone. The address is eleven Lawrence Lane in Riversville."

"Thanks, Old Man," said Rhaymi, walking into the kitchen.

Ken twisted at the waist and touched his toes before sitting back down. Rhaymi bounced back into the room.

"Is he coming?"

"Yeah, he'll be here in about thirty minutes. I woke him up. Oops. My bad. I hate getting woken up early."

"Nobody likes get an early phone call on a Saturday."

"You got that right, Old Man."

Ken stayed in his chair and Rhaymi sat on the floor. The two talked non-stop for thirty minutes, sixty minutes, ninety minutes. Ken hadn't noticed the time until two hours later.

"Whoa, Kiddo. It's been two hours."

"No; it has not."

"Yeah, it has. Two hours."

"Really?"

"Yeah, really. Where's this boyfriend of yours? This is the second time he's been late."

"Well, I woke him up. He probably jumped in the shower. He'll be here soon."

"Nope, sorry, Rhaymi," said Ken, standing and walking with a purpose toward the kitchen. "I already went through this once. I have stuff to do this afternoon. Come on, let's go."

"No, Ken, we have to stay."

Ken wrote on an orange post-it note and peeled it from the stack. He grabbed his keys and opened the door, pressing the note on the door.

"I left a note on the door. If he doesn't like it, too bad. Serves him right for being two hours late."

Rhaymi pleaded in tow, "Ken, can we just stay here? You shouldn't be driving."

"I feel fine. I'll drive you to your dorm. Hop in the car. Let's go."

Chapter 17

Bouncing up and down on his toes, Ken turned toward the loudspeaker at the sound of the announcement: "All runners report to the starting line; all runners report to the starting line. The race will begin in five minutes."

Ken stood under the tent next to the registration table, looking through the hundreds of runners filing toward the marathon's starting line. He looked at his watch, sighed, and began to walk toward the colorful arched banner running from one side of the street to the other.

"Hey, Ken! Kenny!"

A step away from the road, Ken turned and saw Rhaymi waving as she sprinted toward him.

"Hi, Ken. Sorry. I overslept," she said, running up to Ken's side.

"It's OK. Come on, let's get you registered."

Moving toward the registration table, Ken tapped Rhaymi on the right shoulder. She sprung forward a step, getting to the table first. She scribbled her information on the form, and began to pin her number to her jacket.

"Unzip your coat and pin your number to your shirt, in case you take your jacket off. It's cold now, but you'll warm up. You might end up taking your coat off."

"Not your first rodeo, is it?"

"I know a few tricks."

"One minute to race time," came the announcement from the race director over the loudspeaker. "One minute to race time."

"Perfect timing," said Rhaymi as she and Ken made their way to the center of the road for the start.

"Did you bring anything to eat or drink?" Ken asked.

"No, I meant to go to the grocery store before I got here, but I didn't have time."

"OK. Well, there's stuff on the course."

"There's a grocery store on the course?"

"No, there's food and drink on the course."

"I know, Ken. It was a joke. Lighten up, Old Man. This is supposed to be fun; my first marathon."

Bang!

The starting gun sounded, and the 300-plus runners all stepped forward. Rhaymi started sprinting, weaving in-and-out of the crowd despite the pack still being bunched up at the start.

"Rhaymi! Rhaymi, stop!"

Stopping twenty feet ahead, Rhaymi waited for Ken to catch up.

"Rhay, you've got to slow down. This is a marathon, not a sprint."

"I know, Ken. But I'm so excited!"

"Yeah, I know. But do you want to finish?"

"No, Ken. I want to get my nails done. Yes, I want to finish."

"OK, well, if you want to finish you've got to stick with me. Slow and steady, my friend. Slow and steady."

"Slow and steady. Sounds boring, just like you."

"It is boring, just like me, but it will get you to the finish."

Rhaymi tilted her head and fake yawned.

"OK. I'll," Rhaymi loudly snored before continuing, "run like you; slow and steady."

Ken nodded as he unzipped the top of his coat an inch, the field of runners starting to thin.

"If we're going to run this slow, I'm going to get bored. Can I at least tell dirty jokes?"

Ken turned to his right and smirked, looking at Rhaymi's playful expression.

"Lay it on me."

"OK. So the Pope, Devil and this old, boring bastard named Ken walk into a bar … "

Chapter 18

The clear plastic cup bounced off the rim of the blue trashcan onto the gravel on the side of the road.

"You missed," Ken said. "I thought you were going to play in the NBA?"

Rhaymi didn't reply. As the race wore on, she talked less and less.

"Bored?"

Rhaymi looked at Ken and shook her head, which was beginning to drop.

"Stay up straight. Leaning forward wastes energy."

Rhaymi lifted her upper body and returned her look forward.

"You're doing great, Kid. There's mile marker twenty-five," Ken said as he pointed. "You have just a little more than a mile to go. You're going to make it."

Rhaymi nodded and Ken smiled. He knew his wisdom had helped his inexperienced friend near the finish line.

"I'm boiling," Rhaymi wheezed.

"So take off your jacket. Just wrap it around your waist."

Rhaymi unzipped her coat, grabbed the sleeves, and tied it in a knot.

"There. That will make you feel better," Ken said. "Are you going to do a cartwheel at the finish line?"

Rhaymi spit, the saliva sticking to her bottom lip and dripping from her chin to the front of her short sleeve shirt.

"Good one."

"Bite me, Ken," she labored.

Ken smiled, happy he not only was helping a friend finish a marathon, but also finally getting a chance to one-up Rhaymi.

"What's the matter? Can someone not take it?"

"Just bite me, Ken."

Ken's smile widened. He reached back with both of his arms and grabbed Rhaymi by the shoulders.

"If you can't take it, don't ... "

Ken noticed three black-and-blue marks on the back of Rhaymi's left arm, a few inches above her elbow.

"What?"

Ken let go, the smile evaporating from his face.

"Ahh, I ... I don't know."

They took a few more strides.

"You're doing great, Kid. About a mile to go."

Chapter 19

Clang-clang-clang-clang-clang-clang.

A spectator rattled a cowbell as Rhaymi and Ken took their final turn, fifty yards from the finish line.

"Go, Rhaymi. Go," Ken encouraged.

Rhaymi turned toward her running mentor.

"There's the finish. Show 'em what you've got, Kid."

Smiling and looking at the red and white balloons that hovered above the finish line banner, Rhaymi licked her top lip and took off in a sprint. Arms pumping and the soles of her sneakers kicking back, she bolted away from Ken and crossed the finish line, thrusting both of her arms into the air.

Ken jogged to the finish, a content look on his face. He pushed the top-right button on his running watch as he crossed the timing mat. Rhaymi turned and exploded toward Ken, her arms stretched wide. Ken smiled briefly before Rhaymi jumped into his arms, wrapping her legs around him at the waist. Ken stepped back and worked to balance himself. Rhaymi put her feet on the ground, jumping up and down in short bursts as her arms kept Ken pinned to her chest. She planted a full kiss on

Ken's right cheek before releasing her grasp and moving her hands to his shoulders.

"I did it, Ken. I did it. I ran a marathon."

"You sure did. You ran a marathon. Congratulations. You can check that off your bucket list."

"I ran a marathon. And you were right, slow and steady. Who knew boring could ever be a good thing?"

Ken smiled, dropping and shaking his head as Rhaymi put her hands on her hips.

"I hope my boyfriend got a picture of me. He may have missed me. I was flying at the finish, Ken. Flying. I was like, whoosh, whoosh, whoosh," she said, moving her arms slowly in a running motion.

"Is he here?"

"Yeah, he's here someplace," said Rhaymi, looking through the fifty or so people at the finish.

"I'd like to meet him."

"I've told him all about you, even the bad things," Rhaymi said, smacking Ken on the back and winking.

"Here; let's get you a drink."

"Ken, I told you, I don't drink."

"Not that kind of … "

"Gotcha again. Kenny, you gotta wake up. You know, pay attention."

Ken shook his head and smiled as they walked toward a table filled with water, Gatorade and chocolate milk, along with bagels and bananas.

"Help yourself, Rhay."

"Oh my God, I could eat this whole table," said Rhaymi, grabbing a bagel and inspecting it before taking a big bite.

"OK, but if you eat the table, where will we put the food?"

"That's lame, Ken. Pretty lame," Rhaymi responded, chewing on the bagel as Ken smiled.

Ken introduced Rhaymi to a group of local runners he knew, quick to be complimentary of her accomplishment. Rhaymi regularly tugged at the circular medal around her neck, and grabbed Ken's arm and laughed loudly when he said anything funny. Noticing the crowd under the post-race tent had started to thin, Ken looked at his watch, his eyes widening when he saw the time – 2:03. He looked away and then back at his watch, calculating how long ago they had finished.

The last of Ken's friends said goodbye and headed toward their cars.

"Hey, Rhay. Is that boyfriend of yours here? Wasn't he supposed to be at the finish?"

"Yeah. He probably got caught up at work."

"On Sunday?"

"Yeah, he's a really hard worker. He makes *a lot* of money"

"Well, money can't buy happiness."

"Yeah, but it can buy me a trip to Aruba, and that's where I'm headed next weekend."

"Boyfriend?"

"You're pretty quick, Ken."

"So, is your boyfriend going to get here pretty quick or what? Am I driving you back to your dorm again?"

"Calm down, Old Man. I'm sure he'll be here ... " said Rhaymi, pointing both index fingers at Ken, " ... pretty quick."

"Yeah, well, I need to hit the porta-potty ... " Ken rebutted, repeating Rhaymi's double point, " ... pretty quick."

"Ha, good one, Ken. You're catching on. You're a fast learner, for an old bastard."

Ken smirked as he exited the tent and searched for the porta-potties. When he returned to the area, Rhaymi wasn't there. Ken scanned the horizon and saw a white Corvette exit the parking area and drive out of sight. He tugged his chin before shaking his head and slowly walking to his car.

Chapter 20

Dinga-linga-ling!

Ken stood from his faithful recliner and walked into the kitchen, grabbing the phone before it rang a second time.

"Hello."

"Hi, Daddy."

"Hi Sweetie," Ken beamed.

"How are you, Daddy? Are you excited to see us next weekend?"

"Yes, of course. I've been looking forward to it for weeks. The state fair will be in town. I thought we could go over there. I thought Celina might like to see the animals."

"That's a great idea, Daddy. She'd like that."

"Good; good."

"Have you been getting out of the house at all? Been on any hot dates?"

"No, but I have spent some time with this girl."

"Really? How old is she?

"Nineteen."

"Nineteen?! Daddy!!"

"No, it isn't like that. We're just friends. We've done a few things with each other; we ran a marathon together a few weeks ago."

"Really?"

"Yeah, her first one."

"Oh, wow. That's cool."

"Yeah, yeah, but I haven't heard from her since then."

"Did you make any plans?"

"No."

"Did you text or call her?"

"No, I don't have her number."

"Does she have your number?"

"No, I don't think so."

"So, Daddy, if you didn't make plans with each other and you don't have each other's number, why would you be expecting to hear from her?"

"I don't know. I just did."

"I don't know what to tell you, Daddy."

"I'm wondering if something's wrong. Do you think I should go to her dorm to check on her?"

"Her dorm room?"

"Yeah, she's in college at Pynchonton."

"Daddy, that would be kind of creepy, you going to her dorm uninvited."

"You think so?"

"Yeah, don't do that."

"OK, but what if something's wrong?"

"You said she's in college?"

"Yeah."

"Well, it's early May. She might have finals coming up. Our finals are this week. She's probably been studying a lot. Sorry, Daddy, I guess she doesn't have time for a sixty-six-year-old man."

"Yeah, you're probably right."

"So, we'll see you in a week?"

"Sure will, Sweetie. Will James be coming?"

"Nope, this is a busy time of year for him at work. It'll just be me and Celina."

"Sounds good to me. See you soon, Sweetie."

"Bye, Daddy."

Ken hung up the phone and took a step toward the family room before he heard three light taps on his front door. He went the door and pushed the white curtain to the side so he could peek outside. He quickly grabbed the knob and whipped the door open.

"Rhaymi," he said, stunned.

Rhaymi stood still, looking directly into Ken's eyes. Her hair was messed up, out of its typical ponytail. Her black jacket was fully unzipped, and she held her arms crossed in front of her.

"What are you doing here?" Ken asked, concerned.

"Can I come in?" she asked softly.

Ken paused before replying, "Yes, of course."

Stepping back to allow Rhaymi inside, Ken closed the door. He gently placed his hand on the back of Rhaymi's left shoulder. She lurched forward before going into the family room and gingerly sitting on the floor. Ken followed, sitting on the edge of his recliner and leaning forward.

"Rhay, what's the matter?"

Mildly shaking her head, she closed her eyes.

Standing up and reaching out with his arms, Ken said, "Here, let me get your coat."

Bending over, he grabbed the end of Rhaymi's left sleeve and gently pulled, causing Rhaymi to grimace. Ken let go and stepped back, raising his eyebrows.

'I got it," Rhaymi said, slowly taking each arm out of the sleeves.

Her jacket dropped to the floor. Ken bent down and picked it up, placing it on the arm of the couch.

"Rhay, you're hurt."

"I'll be OK."

Ken stared at Rhaymi as she sat uncomfortably on the floor.

"Is it your boyfriend?" Ken asked.

"No."

Ken cautiously walked around his guest, sitting back on the edge of his recliner to look at Rhaymi.

"Come on, Rhay. Tell me the truth. You've been to the hospital with two wrist injuries, you've had your stomach pumped even though you tell me you don't drink, you crashed your car into a tree, I saw bruises on the back of your arm during the marathon, and now this. It's your boyfriend, isn't it? I know it is."

"I deserved it," said Rhaymi, propping herself up and looking at Ken for the first time since entering the family room.

"What?"

"It was my fault. I was making him dinner and I cooked a steak in the stove the wrong way and it starting smoking and the smoke detector went off and the whole house smelled like smoke. It was bad."

"Why were you cooking him dinner at his house?"

"Well, I was just over there. It was dinner time, so I thought I'd make him something."

"So what happened?"

"What do you mean?"

"With your arm; your shoulder there. You're hurt."

"It was just an argument. It's OK."

"No, it's not OK. You're hurt. Do you want me to take you to the hospital?"

"No, I can't go there anymore."

"What?! What do you mean you can't go there anymore?"

"I just can't, Ken. OK?" snapped Rhaymi.

Ken sat back in his chair and examined Rhaymi's face.

"You look tired, Rhay."

Rhaymi dropped her shoulders and let out a sigh.

"I am. I'm exhausted."

"Do you want to stay here? You can stay in my daughter's room. It's all ready. She's coming here next week with my granddaughter."

"I can't stay here, Ken. I have a meeting with a professor tomorrow at nine in the morning, and I have finals the next four days. I have to study. I have to do well on finals or I'm going to get kicked out of the nursing program."

After pacing the room for a moment, Ken said, "That's not a problem. I can drive you to school tomorrow morning, you can go see your professor, you get your books, I'll pick you up, and you can come back and study here for the week. I don't have any big plans. I'm just doing this and that around the house until my daughter comes Friday. She's a professor; English."

"English?" Rhaymi replied, looking at Brooke's high school photograph on the wall. "Wow, she must be smart."

"She is."

"I bet she never failed any finals."

"You're not going to fail. Here, you can sit at the kitchen table, spread all your books out, and do all the studying you want. That's what Brooke used to do. I work mostly in the yard. I won't even be inside."

"Sounds boring, Ken."

"Yeah, it is. But there won't be any distractions."

"I don't know."

"Tell you what – if you stay here, when you're done studying, I'll play you at Uno. I won't beat you too bad. I don't want to be rude, you know, to a guest."

"Those are fightin' words, Ken. Don't make me fight you. I don't wanna whip your butt in your own house."

Ken bent his knees, putting him almost at eye level with Rhaymi. He stuck his hand out.

"Do we have a deal?" Ken smiled.

Rhaymi smirked and paused before grabbing Ken's hand and shaking it.

"OK, Old Man. You've gotta deal."

Chapter 21

The young male security guard at the college's entrance didn't look up as Ken's silver car neared. Ken slowed down, but he hit the speed bump faster than he had hoped.

"Whoops."

"Easy. God, you almost made me fart," said Rhaymi, sticking out her tongue and making flatulent sounds with her mouth, forcing a reluctant smile from her driver.

"Where's your dorm again? I get all twisted around whenever I drive in here."

"It's one way. How can you get twisted around? Geez, you're old. Maybe you shouldn't be driving. Aren't there driving laws for people like you?"

"Where's your building, Missy Pants?"

"Up your butt and to the right."

Ken let out a loud laugh, looking at Rhaymi before shaking his head and putting his eyes back on the road.

"Up here on the left, across from the Jesus statue."

"Amen, Sister."

"Amen, Brother."

Ken smiled again before pulling to the right side of the one-way circular road. Rhaymi hopped out of the car and walked in front of Ken's car toward her dorm. Ken rolled down the passenger side window.

"Rhay, what's your number?" asked Ken.

The two exchanged cell numbers. Ken slowly typed the new number into his flip phone with his right index finger.

"What time do you want me to pick you up?"

"Eleven?"

"OK, right here at eleven. In the morning, right?

"Good one, Ken," said Rhaymi, as she flashed a thumb's up and continued to her dorm.

Ken looked at his watch, which read 8:43.

"OK, I've got a little more than two hours," he said as he watched Rhaymi bounce to the front door of her dorm, a rectangular brick building that matched all of the other structures in sight.

Ken closed his eyes, took a deep breath and slowly exhaled. He opened his eyes, placed his hands back on the steering wheel, and started to drive.

"Time to pay someone a visit."

Chapter 22

The black and white wooden gate lifted as Ken pulled into the private parking lot for Tatum Financial, one of the biggest and wealthiest businesses in Pynchonton. Ken entered the Federal-style structured building, looking at the company names and locations on the board high on the wall in the foyer.

"Fifth floor," he said softly, pushing the number five on the elevator button.

When the metallic doors opened at the fifth floor, a large glass door stood ten feet away, and the words "Tatum Financial", written in gold letters, appeared at eye level. Ken opened the door and was greeted with a big smile by a young, attractive receptionist at the front desk.

"Good morning, Sir. How can we help you today?"

A switch went on in Ken, followed by an ear-to-ear smile.

"Hiiiiiiiii. Wow, your hair looks stunning today. You should be on a catwalk someplace," he said, looking directly at the curly-haired brunette.

"Well, aren't you the nicest thing?"

"Hey, I call 'em how I see 'em."

"Who do you have an appointment with this morning, Sir?"

"Well ... " continued Ken, slowly leaning against the desk while maintaining his eye contact.

"Candace."

"Well, Candace. I just retired and I'm looking for a new financial planner. I plan on living a long time. The ticker's still firing on all cylinders. I want to stay aggressive and make money. I'm looking for a real bulldog; a young buck. Anyone come to mind?"

"Oh, well we have just the person for you, mister ... "

"Ken Roy."

"Well, Mr. Roy. Our clients love one of our new financial planners. He's only been here less than two years, but he's made a lot of money for a lot of people: Mathew O'Donnell."

"Mathew O'Donnell," repeated Ken.

"Yeah, maybe you've heard the name before; football player not too long ago in Heapstown; his dad's been a Pynchonton police officer for a long time."

Freezing for what felt like a lifetime, Ken stared at the receptionist, who held her smile in return.

"Perfect," said Ken, returning to his upbeat tone. "I'm free right now if he's available."

"Well, he has appointments all morning."

Dropping his head, Ken worked to think of a reply.

"But you know, his ten o'clock is usually a little late. You wouldn't believe how many people show up late."

Perking back up, Ken jumped at the opportunity.

"If I told you, Candace, that I could be out of there by 10:05, could you squeeze me in? I just want to say hello, touch base, and then I can make a regular appointment when I leave."

"I don't see why not, Mr. Roy. That seems reasonable."

"You are as kind as you are beautiful, Candace," said Ken, who was far outside of his comfort zone.

"You are a sweetheart, Mr. Roy."

Ken smiled and sat in a black leather wing chair, settling in and thinking of his next, deliberate move.

Chapter 23

Fifty uneventful minutes passed as Ken ran the brief conversation through his head. He wasn't sure what Rhaymi's boyfriend would say, and he believed he would be asked to leave the building within minutes. His message had to be direct.

"Right this way, Mr. Roy," said Candace as she stood and walked down a green-carpeted hall.

Ken stoically followed, his chest out. Candace opened the thick brown door and Ken walked in. He saw a broad-shouldered young man behind a dark wooden desk, wearing a white-collared shirt and a red tie with small gold stars. He swiveled back-and-forth in his black chair while talking on the phone. Ken looked at his black hair, which was gelled and combed to the left. He twirled a pen in his right hand, and his muscular frame was obvious.

'He'll be right with you," Candace whispered as Ken sat down in a maroon wing chair.

Rhaymi's boyfriend hung up the phone and stood, extending his thick hand toward his guest. "Hi. Welcome to Tatum Financial. Mathew O'Donnell," he said confidently, his height catching Ken's attention.

Ken extended his hand and shook the young man's hand, releasing before he replied.

"Ken Roy. I'm friends with Rhaymi."

"Heeeeey, Mr. Roy. It's great to finally meet you. Rhaymi's told me all about you. She hasn't stopped talking about the marathon. She said she never would have made it without you. She said you carried her. I really didn't know what she meant by that until she explained it to me. Our whole trip in Aruba, it was Ken, Ken, Ken."

Ken stood, watching Mathew's demonstrative hand gestures and physical presence.

"So, Mr. Roy, Rhaymi said you recently retired. What do you do for working out other than running? You're obviously in good shape."

Ken paused, staring at the young man's impressive smile.

"Yeah, I run, and bike. I do my planks and some bicep curls."

"You're what we call a young retiree, Mr. Roy."

"Yeah," he answered, cracking a smile. "I guess I am. I feel young, even though Rhaymi calls me Old Man."

"Yeah, that sounds like her," Mathew laughed, shaking his head. "That's one reason why I love her so much; I don't know what words are going to come out of that mouth. She keeps things exciting."

"She's not boring, that's for sure."

"You've got that right, Mr. Roy," laughed Mathew again. "So, how can I help you today?"

Mathew stood, his hands on his hips and his shoulders square to Ken, who paused and searched for the words he had prepared earlier.

"I was in the building. Just wanted to say hi."

Mathew smiled and nodded slightly.

"That's it," continued Ken, sticking out his hand. "Nice meeting you."

The men shook hands, Mathew's smile dominating the room. Ken walked out of the room, down the hall, out the large glass door, and pushed the down arrow for the elevator. The doors opened and Ken stepped forward, pushing the button for the ground level. The elevator doors sealed shut.

Hastily, Ken pushed the circular open door button, and the metallic doors responded immediately. Marching out of the elevator and back onto the fifth floor, he threw the glass door to Tatum Financial open and progressed along the green carpet of the hallway, ignoring Candace. He maintained his stride until he reached Mathew's desk.

"Touch Rhaymi again, and I'll blow your head off."

Mathew, who was still standing, raised his eyebrows. Ken turned and advanced back down the hallway. Keeping his eyes focused forward, he left the office and pushed the tan door for the stairwell open, with the metal handle slamming against the cinderblock wall, creating a thunderous echo. His rubber-soled sneakers tapped on the cement stairs as he made his way down the five flights. He stepped outside, and the morning sun caught his attention. He opened his car door and looked into his eyes in the rearview mirror. He stared and stared and stared.

Chapter 24

To Ken's surprise, Rhaymi showed up on time – exactly at eleven.

"Hey, Old Man," smiled Rhaymi, carrying Freddie in the cat carrier in one hand, and her broken backpack and a small suitcase in the other. "I'm mmmov'in in."

Ken let out a sigh, guessing Mathew hadn't said anything yet to Rhaymi about his trip to the office.

"Got what you need?"

"Yup, I packed my zip ties, shotgun and safe cutter. I'm good to go."

Ken chuckled. He tried to make eye contact with Freddie as he pulled away from the curb.

"So, you can stay at my house all week. There won't be any distractions and … and you're safe. There aren't any problems at my house."

"Oh, there will be, Ken," said Rhaymi, drawing a concerned look from her host. "You're about to have cat piss stains all over the place. Hope you have some rug cleaner."

"Come on, now, I'm serious. You won't have anything to worry about with me. You just have to study. You know, hit the books. And if that boyfriend of yours reaches out to you, you just tell him you don't have time for him right now because you're studying. That's all you have to do – tell him you're studying."

"OK, Ken. I'll tell him I'm studying."

"Atta-girl."

"And Ken, I will make you the best dinners you've ever had. I can cook anything: chicken, steak, pasta, seafood. If nursing doesn't work out, I could be a chef. I'd be a great chef; I mean, *great.*"

"I don't need you to cook for me. I'm a big boy; I can take care of myself. Plus, you're my guest. You don't cook for me; I cook for you."

That evening, Ken prepared his wife's favorite: pasta and meatballs, along with French bread and a salad with Italian dressing. Ken worked on the meal for an hour. He called in Rhaymi, who bounced into the kitchen from the family room and sat down at the small table, speechless. Ken had the table fully set. He brought a plate of pasta to Rhaymi, placed it on the table, looked at his guest, and thought of his wife.

Marie's head was tilted to the left and her eyes looked upward. In her wheelchair at the table, Ken spooned the broth into her mouth, careful not to spill any on the red bib she wore for every meal.

"I added a little pepper to this to give it some flavor. I think you'll like it," Ken kindly said.

Ken's chair fit awkwardly at the table, on the corner. He sat at the edge of his seat, his back upright and his moves deliberate.

"Do you like it?" asked Ken, looking into his wife's brown eyes as he stirred the soup. "It shouldn't be too hot. I put an ice cube in it."

A faint sound came from Marie, whose only movements came from her lips and throat.

"Everyone from the office says 'hi'. They miss you. They say the place isn't the same without Marie's special touch," continued Ken, picking up a white napkin and dabbing his wife's chin. "Doreen showed me how to text. I think I finally got it figured out, probably ten years later than everyone else. I see all the kids texting. I figure Celina will be texting someday. I thought she would think it was cool if her Grampy knew how to text."

Marie's head rolled to the right and then back into its position on the left.

"OK, more soup. You got it," said Ken, scooping another spoonful out of the bowl and raising it to Marie's mouth.

Bang!

The plates and silverware rattled on the kitchen table at the force of Rhaymi's hands striking the table top.

"This is the best sauce, Ken. The best. What's in it?" she asked.

"Oh, that's Marie's family recipe – got it from her great-grandmother."

"It's the best. Has a little punch. Boom, boom, boom," said Rhaymi, playfully punching Ken on the left bicep. "Let me tell you, all this studying, and this sauce, I'm acing my finals. Acing them."

Ken smiled and shook his head, happy to see Rhaymi energetic and happy.

"You don't believe me, do you?"

"No, no, I believe you," smiled Ken.

"No you don't. Here, I'll prove it to you."

Rhaymi sprang up, the metal-legged chair shuffling across the floor. In two long strides she left the room. She returned immediately, rocketing back into the kitchen and slapping a two-inch thick pile of index cards on the table.

"Hit me, Old Man. I know every answer."

Slightly taken aback for a moment, Ken grabbed the top card.

"Name the antidote for warfarin?" he asked.

"Vitamin K!" Rhaymi blurted. "Haha. Another one."

"Name the valve a nurse would be hearing when auscultating over the second right intercostal space," Ken said with a frown.

"Aortic!" came Rhaymi's sudden response. "I'm acing my finals, Kenny. Come on, another one."

Ken lifted the index card and read another question. He did so for the next two hours, the dirty dishes still on the kitchen table.

"OK, that's all of them. You went through the whole pile. You got them all right."

"Except for the one about hollow breathing sounds," said Rhaymi, tapping the table with her right hand. "I'm so stupid."

Ken paused before replying, "Stupid? Kid, you just answered, I don't know, hundreds and hundreds of questions, and you got them all right except one."

"I can't believe I missed that one. I'm such an idiot."

"You missed one question. Who cares? You're smart, Kid, and I mean *really* smart."

"Thanks, Ken," said Rhaymi, smiling and rubbing her right hand along her host's left forearm. "You're so sweet. You always make me feel good. I bet you were such a good dad."

Ken stood, grabbed Rhaymi's plate and silverware, and put it in the sink. He turned and leaned up against the counter.

"Rhay, can I ask you a question?"

"Sure, let me go get more index cards," she said, springing from her chair.

"No, no, not a nursing question. A, ahh, personal question."

"Fire away, Kenny boy."

"Dad. You've never mentioned your Dad, or your Mom for that matter. Can I ask why?"

"I've never met my Dad, and my mom lives in Malibu," she said matter-of-factly. "She's a realtor."

"You've never met your Dad?"

"Nope. Don't know who he is."

"You don't know who he is?

"Nope. I think my mom had a fling and got pregnant. She never really told me what happened."

"Never told you? Why don't you ask her?"

"We don't talk much."

"Oh. Well, when was the last time you talked to her?"

"I don't know."

"You don't know? What do you mean you don't know?"

"Really, I don't know."

"Take a guess."

"I don't know. I think when I came here for college."

"When you came here for college? You serious?"

"Yeah."

"That was … " Ken paused and counted on his fingers, " … twenty-one months ago?"

"Yeah, that sounds right."

"Didn't you go home for Christmas?"

"No, I couldn't afford a flight home, so I stayed at my boyfriend's house."

"Couldn't afford a flight home?"

"Yeah, I didn't have enough money."

"What about for the summer?"

"I stayed here. My boyfriend got me a job filing papers at his office."

"You didn't go home at all? You have, what is it, two or three months off?"

"No, I stayed here and worked. I didn't mind. Mathew and I went to the Cape every weekend. His parents have a place in Hyannis Port. I could walk to the beach."

"The beach. Well, that sounds nice."

"It was. The beach, every weekend. We always went out, and went to so many cool places."

'Sounds like a fun summer."

'Yeah, it was."

Ken grabbed his plate and glass and placed it in the sink, hesitating before turning around. "Rhay, I'm sorry, why didn't your Mom pay for your flight home?"

'She said it was my decision to go to college this far away, so if I wanted to come home I had to pay for it myself."

"Well, it does cost a lot to go to Pynchonton College. What is it, something like $20,000?"

"Try fifty-five big ones, Ken."

"Fifty-five thousand dollars?" Ken spouted.

"Yup, but I don't pay that. I don't pay anything. I got a full scholarship."

"Full scholarship?"

"Yup. I'm wicked smaht, Ken. Wicked smaht," said Rhaymi, giving her best New England accent.

"Wow, you must be smart to get a full scholarship. For academics, right?"

"No, Ken. Hopscotch."

Smiling, Ken pushed himself off the counter and picked up the rest of the dishes from the table.

"Woah, what's today? Monday, right?" Ken asked.

"That's what the calendar says."

"Almost forgot. I have to put the trash out."

"Sounds exciting, Ken. I'll alert the authorities."

Ken shook his head, his eyes twinkling as he pulled the trash bag out of the bin under the sink. He moved from room to room, emptying the small baskets into the large bag. When he came downstairs Rhaymi was back sitting on the floor in the family room, leaning forward and writing on flashcards.

Ken quietly walked by, seeing the focus on Rhaymi's face. Trash bag in hand, he walked into the garage, dropped the bag in the big blue bin and pushed the button to open the garage door. As the large door opened, he saw a car slowly driving toward his house from the left. The vehicle's brake lights came on, and the car stopped at the end of Ken's driveway.

Chapter 25

The passenger side window on the shiny SUV rolled all the way down. Ken didn't recognize the vehicle, and his outdoor floodlight wasn't powerful enough to reveal the driver.

"Hey, stranger," the driver called.

Ken, pulling his big blue bin toward the end of the driveway, cautiously moved forward, ducking to try to get a better look inside.

"Who is that?" he asked.

"Geraldo Rivera."

Ken squinted and stepped forward, standing up and letting out a laugh.

"I didn't recognize you," Ken said. "When did you get this? Looks sharp."

"Yesterday afternoon," replied Robbie Flanagan, his longtime neighbor. "It's probably the last car I'll have before I go into the home, so I thought I'd make it count."

Ken laughed again, "Yeah, you and me both."

"When did Brooke get in?"

"What's that?"

"When did Brooke get in? Mae said she saw her outside your house this morning."

"Brooke? No, she comes this weekend."

"Son of a gun, I knew it, my wife's losing her mind."

"Ohhh, no. Mae probably saw me with this girl I know."

"Hey, Ken. Back in the ballgame. Good for you."

"No, it's a girl. She's in college at Pynchonton."

Robbie raised his eyebrow and grinned at his friend, "College girl? Didn't know you still had that in you, Ken."

"No, no. It's not like that at all, Robbie."

Ken turned and looked back at the front door, letting go of the bin and leaning on his friend's car door.

"I met her when I was volunteering at the hospital," Ken explained. "She's a really good kid. She has a ton of energy, and she's funny, and she's as smart as they come. But she's involved with this guy – Mathew O'Donnell."

"Oh yeah, police captain's son; he was Heapstown's running back when they won the states a few years ago. I've met that kid a few times. I don't trust him. Something about him."

"Yeah, well, I think he's abusing her. She's been to the hospital a few times, and I saw some bruises on her once, and she knocked on my door last night scared to death. She's a million miles away from home. There's no dad, and her mom doesn't seem too interested in her either. She's a good kid but ... "

"Maybe get her some counseling," Robbie interjected.

"What's that?"

"Counseling; some therapy."

"Therapy."

"Yeah, did wonders for me. I was killing myself at work, carrying the weight of the world on my shoulders. It's not easy being in charge of a newspaper, Ken. But once I went to therapy, my whole life changed. All the pressure came off and all the distractions went away."

"Distractions. That's it; she has too many distractions."

"Take her to Dr. Jonassen on School Street. Laura's great. She's really easy to talk to."

"All right, that sounds good."

Ken stepped back and grabbed the handle to the trash container.

"Hey, you guys printing any fake news tomorrow?"

"Nope. But if we were, Ken, I wouldn't tell you."

Ken smiled and waved to his neighbor, who slowly pulled away. Putting the bin in its place along the curb, Ken walked back toward his garage, looking at his front door.

"Not sure how this is going to go over."

Chapter 26

A bell on the back of the white door jingled, the sound repeating as Ken closed the door to Dr. Jonassen's office. A man in his mid-thirties with dark brown hair sat in one of the four chairs, his legs crossed and his eyes closed behind his glasses. Ken sat quietly in the chair closest to the door, doing his best not to disturb the man. He waited uncomfortably for a minute, then another, in the small waiting area. The room, undecorated with off-white walls, was perfectly silent.

The interior door opened. A lanky bald man, maybe fifty, Ken estimated, stepped into the room, his eyes bloodshot.

"See you next week," said a female voice.

Ken turned to see a well-dressed slender woman in her fifties.

"William, come on in."

The gentleman in the chair stood up, keeping his eyes closed until he took his first step and entered the office.

"Can I help you?"

Ken hesitated. The unexpected movement, while subtle, caught him off guard. The lady looked at Ken, the kindness in her eyes apparent.

"Dr. Jonassen?"

"Yes, I'm Dr. Jonassen."

"My neighbor, Robbie Flanagan, suggested I come see you."

"OK. So you need to make an appointment?"

"I, ahh, actually, it's not for me; it's for a friend. There's this girl, a college kid, I met, and she, um, well she's in a bad relationship with this guy. She's a good kid, but, um, he doesn't treat her right. I think … I think he does things to her."

"That sounds serious."

"Oh, I think it is."

"OK, well unfortunately if she wants an appointment she needs to contact me herself."

"Oh. I, ahh, I don't know if she'll do that."

"How come?"

"Well, this guy, she just doesn't see that he's bad for her. I went to talk to her last night about it, but I chickened out."

"OK, well, I'm sorry, but to get an appointment she needs to contact me."

"Yeah, OK. I guess that makes sense."

Ken reached for the doorknob and turned the handle, the bell jingling again.

"We do have a support group for victims of abuse."

Ken turned, his eyebrows raised.

"What's that?"

"We have a support group. We meet on Fridays at four in the afternoon for an hour. You don't need an appointment for that, and anyone is welcome to join us."

"Anyone? So I could come with Rhay ... with my friend?"

"Absolutely. In fact, we encourage people to bring friends and family. It gives the victims a sense of support and educates more people about abusive relationships."

"Fridays at four?"

"Yes, Sir. Friday at four."

"OK, then. See you Friday at four."

Chapter 27

The two plastic bags banged into the screen door as Ken reached for the black handle, his left arm corralling a completely filled paper bag. He placed the groceries on the table and walked into the family room, where Rhaymi again had the floor covered with index cards.

"I know 'em all, Kenny. Every single one," she said, partially covering her mouth and changing her tone. "Nurse Summers, Nurse Summers; report to the ER."

Ken smiled, and his eyes softened.

"If you turn a fan on, I'll kill you; I'll kill you right in your own living room."

Ken laughed, leaving the room and going back into the kitchen. Rhaymi skipped in tow.

"What's in the bags? Any tampons? I'm starting to run a little low."

"What's the saying you kids use: TMI?"

"Wow, Ken. Good one. LOL," she said, poking her finger three times into the back of Ken's shoulder.

"Yeah, well, I can't tell if you're serious or not, but if you're serious there's probably some stuff in my daughter's room, in her closet. Help yourself."

"She's coming Friday?"

"Yeah. I'm looking forward to seeing her and my granddaughter. I haven't seen them in a few months."

"When was the last time you saw her?"

"In December, at her mom's funeral."

"Oh, Ken. I'm sorry."

"Nothing to be sorry about. You just asked a question. You didn't know."

"I'm always saying stupid things."

"I don't think you say stupid things. I think you're really smart. I couldn't memorize all those cards you have on the floor in there," continued Ken, pointing toward the family room.

"No, I just need to learn to shut my fucking mouth."

"Rhay!" Ken said, surprised. "What are you talking like that for? I've never heard you say anything like that."

"I'm sorry."

"It's OK. I just … wasn't expecting it. Plus, you're smart. You don't need to talk like that."

"I'm sorry," she repeated, sprawling her hands out on the kitchen table and laying her head down.

Ken examined her, trying to piece together the last few seconds.

"Hey, Rhay. I, um, wanted to talk to you about something."

"Fire away, Ken," she answered blandly, not moving.

"I went to see a therapist today. She was recommended to me by my neighbor."

Rhaymi slowly rose, crossing her arms in front of her chest

"A therapist? Ken, you're, like, the most normal person on the face of the earth. Plus, you're boring. Boring people don't see therapists. Why are you seeing a therapist?"

"Oh, no. I'm not seeing one; I just went to talk to her."

"What about?"

Ken stopped, placed his hands on the kitchen counter and leaned backward. He scratched the back of his head, his nose curling.

"Ahh, well, she has this group therapy on Fridays, and I thought, well, I was wondering if you wanted to go with me?"

Rhaymi stood up, placing her hands on her hips.

"What kind of group therapy?"

Ken sensed a change in Rhaymi's tone. He pushed himself off the counter, looked her in the eyes, and took three cautious steps forward.

"Rhay, do you trust me?"

"What?"

"Do you trust me?"

"You aren't going to do anything weird, are you?"

"No," he said, confused. "Good God, do you trust me?"

Rhaymi dropped her shoulders and relaxed.

"Of course I trust you, Ken. You're the most trustworthy, boring person I know."

"Rhay, you have to believe me when I tell you this," explained Ken, gently putting his hands on the outside of his guest's shoulders. "You're mixed up with the wrong guy."

Lowering her head, Rhaymi released a sigh.

"A bad guy; a dangerous guy," Ken continued. "Look how great you're doing here, and it's because you don't have Mr. Corvette jerking you around."

"He's not as bad as you make him out to be."

"Rhay, something tells me he's even worse than I could imagine."

Rhaymi bit her bottom lip and looked at the floor. Ken, his hands still on Rhaymi's shoulders, bent his knees a notch, trying to make eye contact.

"Rhay."

She responded by looking up, lifting her eyebrows and looking away to the right.

"He tells me all the time he loves me."

Ken waited a moment before responding, "Saying he loves you only means something if he shows you he loves you."

Rhaymi lifted her right hand, wiping away a tear from just below her eyelid.

"Rhay, I was married to my wife for forty-five years. She was the best thing that ever happened to me. I know what love is, Rhay, and this guy doesn't love you."

Rhaymi quickly lifted both of her hands and covered her eyes, the tears running down her face. Ken, lowering his knees a little more, continued to make eye contact.

"Would you like a hug?"

Pausing for a second, Rhaymi nodded, keeping her hands over her eyes as she fought to keep herself from crying out loud. Ken slowly leaned in and gently wrapped his arms around Rhaymi. Ken kept his head up and was careful not to squeeze too tightly.

"Do you want to go to group therapy with me Friday?"

Staying in Ken's protective and fatherly arms, Rhaymi quickly nodded.

"OK, then. It's a date, but not a weird date."

Chapter 28

Freddie meowed as he sat in his cat carrier on Rhaymi's lap in Ken's car.

"You can stay at my place," Ken pleaded as he drove Rhaymi to her college for her final two exams on Friday. "We have room."

"No, Ken. Your daughter and granddaughter are coming to visit. That's a special time for all of you. I don't want to be a third wheel."

"You wouldn't be. I think we'd all get along fine."

"I've been staying in her room. She's going to think I'm weird."

"No, she's not. Hey, how about you sleep in my bed?"

Rhaymi turned toward Ken and curled her nose.

"No. Come on. I mean you can sleep in my room and I'll sleep on the couch. I don't sleep much anyway. I won't even know the difference."

"Ken, I can't take your room and sleep in your bed. I could never do that to someone. That's not right. Plus, you need some father-daughter and father-granddaughter time. How many months ago did you see them?"

"I don't know, four or five - in December."

"Yeah, see, I'm not getting in the way of your time with your family. Don't worry, Kenny, we'll catch up," Rhaymi said, slapping Ken's right thigh as he drove. "We're buddies."

"All right, but I'm still picking you up for therapy today. There's no backing out of that. You said you'd go."

"Yeah, yeah."

"Yeah, well, I'll yeah yeah you at 3:45 in front of the Jesus statue."

"OK," Rhaymi said, sticking her fingers into her cat carrier.

"And if your boyfriend reaches out to you, just don't reply. Or tell him you have two finals today and can't talk. No, five finals."

"No one has five finals in a day. Get with the program."

"OK, well then tell him two, because that's true. Or just don't reply. That's the best thing. Don't reply. Cut him off. You can do so much better than him."

"Yeah," said Rhaymi as she looked out the window. Ken's car turned onto the campus. Ken smiled and waved to the guard inside the security gate and, once again, he hit the speed bump too fast.

"If you hurt Freddie, I'll have to kill ya. Just sayin'."

"Yeah yeah."

"I need to get Freddie a helmet when he rides with crazy Kenny, don't I Freddie?" Rhaymi said, lifting the cat carrier, her lips gently touching the plastic.

Ken stopped the car in front of Rhaymi's dorm. She grabbed the handle to Freddie's carrier and plucked her backpack and suitcase out of the backseat. Then she closed the door with her foot and walked toward the stone building.

"You good?" asked Ken. He was standing next to his car with the door open, talking over the vehicle.

Rhaymi half-turned and nodded, keeping her stride.

"Hey, 3:45. Right here," Ken added.

Rhaymi did a pirouette. Then she stopped and bowed, facing Ken, before finishing her spin and walking to the portico of the building.

Chapter 29

"Flight 303 to Amsterdam, now boarding; Flight 303 to Amsterdam, now boarding."

Sitting in the baggage claim area of New England Airport thirty minutes before Brooke and Celina were scheduled to land, Ken looked toward the voice from the intercom. Years before his retirement, he and Marie had planned to go to Amsterdam the first summer of their retirement from Huber. Neither of them had ever traveled outside of the United States, except for a trip to Canada for Quebec City's Winter Carnival.

Even with Marie's ALS, Ken thought a quick, simple trip to The Netherlands was feasible. In his mind, it would be worth his efforts.

However, those travel plans, along with all of their retirement plans, changed when Ken took Marie to her doctor in late November. Dr. Toman, in her mid-sixties herself and Marie's doctor for thirty years, was concerned mainly for Ken, who had taken a month off from work in order to care for his wife, who needed 24/7 attention. The other concern was Marie's ability to eat. She was having difficulty swallowing and, despite Ken's efforts, just wasn't taking in enough food. Dr. Toman admitted Marie to Pynchonton Senior Care at the hospital, where she received constant care and had her own room for the next twenty-seven days.

"Hi, Sweetheart. My, don't you look beautiful today," said Ken as he walked into his wife's room, opening the curtains to let in some natural light. "Did you sleep well last night?"

Marie didn't budge. Her ability to move was nearly completely absent.

"Hey, Sweetheart. We're still on for The Netherlands. I was thinking we could go in May. Here, I want to show you something."

Ken opened a manila folder he was carrying and took out a number of pieces of paper.

"Look at these. I printed them off the internet," Ken smiled, organizing the papers neatly. "Doreen came over and helped me. She found this really nice website about The Netherlands. It was in Dutch. We couldn't read a thing, but then she saw the translate button and, *voila*, it was in English. What will they think of next?"

Licking his right index finger and thumb, he plucked the first picture off the top of the pile and put it close to Marie's face.

"Look at this," Ken said with excitement. "So, you know how Amsterdam is filled with canals, right? Well, they have these canal tours. You pay twenty-five euros - I don't know how much American money that is, but I'm sure it's not a lot - and you can tour the whole city on a boat on the canal. Isn't that amazing? I'm sure we could get your wheelchair on there. We could ... we could see everything, just like we were walking around."

Ken placed the picture on the white sheet of the bed.

"Oh, and here's a good one," he continued, holding another paper photograph inches from Marie's eyes. "Check this out – a real castle. It's called Muidenslot. It has a drawbridge and a moat, just like in the movies. We'd have to drive there, but I think we could do it. Can you imagine us going over a drawbridge into a castle in Europe?"

"And I saved the best for last," he smiled, placing a photo filled with tulips on the bed. "May is the best time of year to see the tulips. There's a gigantic tulip garden outside of Amsterdam. I'm sure we could find it."

Ken's eyes twinkled, and he looked at Marie. She hadn't moved or made a sound since he arrived.

###

Ken slapped his left thigh, feeling something move. His flip phone was vibrating. He stood to take it out of his pocket, fumbling to push the correct button to answer.

"Hello," he said, startled.

"Hi, Daddy."

"Oh, hi Sweetie. Are you here? Did you land already?"

"No, Daddy. We're boarding now. Our connecting flight from BWI was delayed. We should land around 3:15."

"Did you say 3:15?"

"Yeah, that's what they just announced."

"Oh. Oh, OK. Alright, well, I'm already here. Celina holding up OK?"

"Yup, she's been easy to travel with so far."

"Good; good. Tell her Grampy can't wait to see her, OK? I'll see you when you get here."

"Bye, Daddy."

"Bye, Sweetie."

Ken pushed the button on his flip phone and looked up. He stuck his thumb out, and then his index finger. He shook his head.

"This won't work. I can't make it."

Sitting back down, he placed his right hand over his mouth, spreading his fingers.

"Shoot," Ken said before standing up. "Shoot."

Ken paced briefly before taking his flip phone out of his pocket and placing it to his left ear after pushing the buttons. He paused.

"Ahhhh," he stumbled. "Hi, Rhay, it's me, Ken. Hey, my daughter's flight is late, and I can't pick you up. I still want to go, I just can't get her back to my house and pick you up and make it for four o'clock at the doctor's office. So here's what I want you to do: call a taxi, or your Yuber thing, and meet me there at four. It's on School Street in Riversville. Dr. Jonassen. They should be able to find it. OK? So meet me there at four. OK, see you then."

Scanning the area, Ken found a large screen high on a wall that displayed the departures and arrivals. His eyes scrolled down the alphabetical list.

"BWI, BWI, BWI," he whispered.

The arrival time read 3:15. Lifting the end of the left sleeve of his jacket, Ken's watch read 2:15. For the next hour, he paced in front of the screen, looking up often for any news. It didn't come until 3:16, when his daughter's flight changed to "Arrived" on the screen.

"Finally."

Ken spotted Brooke pushing Celina in a stroller toward the baggage claim area. He clapped his hands once and waved his hands over his head, smiling as he walked in his daughter's direction.

"Hi, Daddy," Brooke beamed.

"Oh, Sweetie, it's great to see you," Ken said as he hugged his daughter, tilting her slightly side-to-side.

"You look good, Daddy."

"Thanks," he said before he pointed at Celina. "Geez, she's out like a light. Did she sleep like that on the plane, too?"

"Nope. She fell asleep right before we landed. She was good on the plane, though. I kept her busy."

"Oh, good. So, Sweetie, we have to get going. I have an appointment at four I don't want to miss, and I want to drive you home first."

Ken turned and looked behind him, hearing the belt move as the luggage began to appear. "Oh, great. There's the luggage."

Brooke followed Ken as he quickly walked toward the belt.

"Which ones are yours?" he asked, looking back at Brooke, who pushed the stroller.

"I don't see them yet," said Brooke, who caught up to her dad at the edge of the belt.

Ken earnestly looked for the right luggage.

"Daddy, I'm surprised you made an appointment for this afternoon when you knew we were coming. That's not like you."

Hearing the concern in his daughter's voice, he slowed his frantic pace.

"Yeah, I'm sorry. It came up at the last second. It wasn't planned."

"Does this have to do with that girl?"

"Noooooo. Well, yeah. It does. She's ... she's going through a real tough time. She's a good kid. She's just ... I don't know. I'm just trying to help her get back on her feet."

"Has she asked you for any money?"

"What?"

"Money. Has she asked you for money, or had you buy her things?"

"No. I bought her some food and some other things when she was staying at the house."

"She stayed at the house? For how many hours?"

"I don't know. Um, five days."

"Five days?!"

"Yeah, she just showed up on Sunday, right after you called."

"Showed up?"

"Yeah. Knocked on the front door."

"Daddy, I think this girl is using you."

"Using me?"

"Yeah, sounds like she wants something."

"No. No, Sweetie. You've got it all wrong. I asked her to stay at the house; she didn't ask to stay."

"I don't know, Daddy. Something doesn't seem right. Oh," pointed Brooke, "there's our bags – the three blue ones."

Reaching as soon as he could, Ken pulled the bags off the belt, flinging one onto his shoulder and carrying the other two.

"OK, gotta hustle," said Ken, looking at his watch as he walked toward the door. "I can't be late for this meeting."

Chapter 30

The bell on the door jingled, louder than Ken recalled three days earlier. With one foot still outside, he suddenly stopped. There was no one in the room.

"Do I have the wrong day?" he wondered.

Looking at his leather-strapped watch, it read 4:01. He stepped fully inside, scratching his head as he looked around the small waiting area. The wooden door opened. Dr. Jonassen stood with a welcoming smile.

"Hello. You're here for the group therapy, right?" she asked.

Ken sighed before replying, "Yes. Yes, thank you."

Walking into Dr. Jonassen's office, he saw a small group of people – three women and one man. Ken hesitated, not seeing Rhaymi. He quickly pulled his cell phone out of his left front pocket and saw that there were no messages.

"Please, have a seat. We were just about to start," Dr. Jonassen said kindly.

Ken sat on a white plastic folding chair, his face puzzled.

"You looked concerned," Dr. Jonassen softly said.

"I'm expecting someone."

"OK. Hopefully they'll be here soon," said Dr. Jonassen as she sat behind her desk.

Ken nodded and relaxed the expression on his face.

"Here, let's begin. This is our therapy group for victims of abuse. My goal for today is for you to know, by the time you leave, that you are not alone. Being a victim of abuse can be isolating. It's important you know there are many, many people in similar situations as you. I encourage you to speak, be honest, take in what others have to say, and recognize you are not alone."

A young woman who Ken guessed to be around thirty, started to cry. Tears made their way through her clenched eyes and down her young face. Dr. Jonassen stood and offered the auburn-haired woman a box of tissues from across her desk. Ken sprang from his chair and handed the tissues to the lady, who stayed seated with her head down.

"That's actually a good start," Dr. Jonassen said. "You're revealing your true emotions, probably for the first time in a while."

The woman snatched a tissue from the box before grabbing it from Ken and placing it on her lap, her pants-covered legs tightly squeezed together.

"Tracy, you've been here before. Can you start us off today, please, if you're comfortable doing so?" asked Dr. Jonassen, looking at a woman seated on the right side of the couch.

"Of course. Hi everyone. My name is Tracy. I'm forty-three years old. I have three children, two in college and one in high school. I'm a stay-at-home-mom and I've been in an abusive relationship for twenty-two years."

Ken's eyebrows rocketed toward the sky.

"My husband is a great provider for our family. We live in Heapstown and also have a second home at the Cape. My husband is a passionate man. He's never struck me; he usually just grabs my shoulders, or pins my arms down in bed. He forces or tricks me to have sex with him, especially oral sex. I do it. He gives me an allowance every week, and at the end of the week I give him the receipts with the total highlighted in yellow and any change left over.

"I first came to Dr. Jonassen four months ago. I couldn't find a receipt. I searched and searched, but I couldn't find it. I knew what was missing: it was a grocery bill. Our youngest son was having his soccer team over for a pasta party the day before a game. He told me at the last second. I rushed to the store to get what was needed, and then I rushed home and got it ready. I must have lost track of it in the process. Anyway, at the end of the week I couldn't find it. When I explained what happened to my husband, he got nose-to-nose with me and told me if I ever lost a receipt again he would kick me out of the house. I love my family and I'll do everything I can to keep us together, so that's why I originally made an appointment for some counseling. I came here because I was afraid of losing my family, but it wasn't until I came and talked to Dr. Jonassen week-after-week that I learned I was in an abusive relationship."

"Well-articulated, Tracy. You've come a long way since our first session. Thank you for sharing that with all of us."

"Would you like us to share something with the group, in front of everyone?" asked the other male, in his mid-twenties.

"Ideally, yes, if you would like to," Dr. Jonassen smiled. "But you don't have to."

"Oh. OK. I don't have anything thought out. I'm only here because my mom begged me to come. Do I have to say my name?"

"No, not at all. You say whatever you're comfortable saying."

"OK, well my mom says I should break up with my girlfriend. My mom said she's *jerking me around*," said the young man, using air quotes. "But I don't think so. I love my girlfriend."

Dr. Jonassen paused before asking, "Why does your mom think that – that your girlfriend is jerking you around, as she says?"

"I don't know. She told me yesterday to come see you. One of her friends has been to you before, I guess."

"Why yesterday?" asked Dr. Jonassen.

"I don't know. I punched a hole in a wall at home."

"Why did you do that?"

"I don't know. I was mad."

"At what?"

The young man hesitated, sitting all the way back before leaning forward and looking at the front of Dr. Jonassen's desk.

"My girlfriend went out to dinner with her ex-boyfriend."

"Does she do that a lot?"

"Um, once in a while."

"And how long has this been going on?"

"I don't know; three years, since we started going out."

"Three years?"

"Yeah. I've kinda gotten used to it. I mean, I don't want to tell her what to do. It's a free country."

"That's very understanding of you. So what made yesterday different; what made you get mad?"

"Well, I texted her after I thought she'd be done with dinner, and she didn't reply. So then I drove over to her apartment, but she wasn't there; I drove to her ex-boyfriend's apartment and I didn't see her car; I drove to her parents' house and her car wasn't there; I texted her best friend and she said she didn't know where she was and that I should let it go.

"I hardly slept. I skipped work and drove to her apartment in the morning. Her car was there so I went and knocked on the door. She answered. I asked her why she didn't reply to my text messages and she said her phone has been acting weird lately. I asked her where she was last night, and she said she was at her apartment. I told her I drove by a little before midnight and her car wasn't there, so where was she? She said I was overreacting, and she had to go to get ready for work and that she would text me later. That's when I went home and punched the wall."

Dr. Jonassen gave a small smile and tilted her head slightly to the right.

"How many times has that happened - your girlfriend going out with her ex-boyfriend?" she asked.

"I don't know; I think that was the eighteenth time."

"And you've told her this bothers you?"

"Yeah."

"And not replying to you, has she done that, too?"

"Yeah, but don't get me wrong. I love my girlfriend. I've asked her to marry me."

"You asked your girlfriend to marry you?"

"Yup."

"And what did she say?"

"She said she'd let me know. She just wants to think about it a little while."

The room was silent, but only for a moment.

"Kid, dump her and get a new girlfriend," said the other woman at the therapy session. "And you, Tracy, you and your asshole husband just need to sign up for marriage counseling. I'm not saying both of you don't have problems, but when it comes to abusive relationships, you guys are in the minor leagues.

"This guy," the woman confidently continued, directing her right thumb at herself, "this guy is a pro."

Dr. Jonassen's eyebrows raised, just a sliver, with her hands perfectly folded on her desk.

The lady sat on the left side of the couch, her left elbow on the furniture's arm. Her legs were crossed, her right foot bouncing, bringing attention to her knee-high leather boots just below her tan skirt. Her tight-fitted white shirt was buttoned to the top, and her highlighted brown hair rested on her narrow shoulders.

"I guess that means it's my turn, doesn't it, Doc?" she asked. "OK, let's crank things up a few notches."

Everyone sat motionless as the lady leaned forward.

"I'm Steph. I'm fifty-two years old. I have no children. I make more than $200,000 a year, and I have for the last ten years. I work from home and out of my company's headquarters in Boston. I've traveled to Europe, Australia and South America. I can't tell you how many times I've gone on cruises in the Caribbean because I've been on so many. I've been to four Super Bowls and four World Series, and I've shaken hands with I don't know how many CEO's of Fortune 500 companies."

Dr. Jonassen nodded slightly.

"Well, boys and girls," Steph continued, her story taking over the room, "my life has been hell; fucking hell. I was in an abusive relationship for thirty-four years, since I was 18. My once wonderful boyfriend-turned-narcissistic-husband has broken my collarbone, wrist, and both arms. I've had at least six concussions; it became hard to tell after a while. I've been thrown against walls, locked in rooms, locked out of rooms, and forced to have sex, although at a bit different level, I'd say, than a few can-you-help-me blowjobs like Tracy. I've been tied up, handcuffed, slapped, choked, and had my hair pulled – all during sex."

"That's awful," Tracy said in a high-pitched voice.

"It was," Steph replied, not missing a beat. "But ya know, the physical abuse wasn't the worst part. I could handle that; I could always bounce back from that. It was the verbal abuse and the manipulation that was the hardest. He had a way of just breaking me down. One time - actually a lot of times - he'd say he'd be home at a certain time and that we could go out, so I'd get al ready. Well, he'd show up an hour, two hours, three hours later, without letting me know. I'd ask him where he'd been or why he didn't text, and he'd tell me I was making too big of a deal out of it, and that I always blow things out of proportion. By the end of it all I'd be the one apologizing and crying, and then giving him a blowjob in the car with his hand on the back of my head.

"How do you like that one, Tracy?" Steph smirked at Tracy, whose mouth dropped open.

"Steph, easy," Dr. Jonassen said softly.

"Sorry," Steph replied, putting her hands up. "I didn't mean anything by it. Sorry, Tracy."

"It's OK," responded Tracy, whose eyes filled with tears.

"I think the worst day, or at least the most bizarre day, came two years ago, the night of my fiftieth birthday. My husband said he'd definitely be home by six and we'd go out to my favorite restaurant. So, I got all dressed up, put on a silk dress I knew he liked, did my hair up just how he liked it, and made sure I was ready before six, just in case he got home early.

"Well, he pulled in a little before eight, and I let him have it right when he opened the door. Effen-this, effen-that. My hands were flying all over the place; I put my finger right in his face. And then he slams the door closed and starts in. We were going at it, I mean, hollering at the top of our lungs, right nose-to-nose. Well, he smacks me on the side of the head, and I go flying into the wall. I grabbed what was there and threw it at him. It was the coats that were hanging on the wall. He started laughing and pointing at me.

"I lost total control of my actions at that point. I really don't remember what I did, but, well, I don't know. It was ... it was just crazy."

"Did anything else happen?" Dr. Jonassen probed.

"Well, our neighbor – good guy - happened to be outside. Apparently, I ran out of the house screaming, in my dress and pumps and got into my car. I drove forward, didn't even back up, and drove across our lawn into the road. He said it was like something you'd see on a TV show. Anyway, he said once I got into the road I gunned it. We live near a T intersection. There's usually a metal guardrail there, but the town was doing some construction at the intersection so there were a bunch of orange barrels. My neighbor said I didn't slow down; I blasted right through two barrels and into a cornfield on the other side of the road. It was late in the fall so there wasn't any corn, just a bunch of dirt and mud. I eventually got stuck. My neighbor said I got out and just started running. I really don't remember. He got in his car and found me running down a road on the other side of the cornfield, with my pumps in my hand. I got into his car, I guess, and he brought me back home. I got out and ran up to a tree in our yard and started punching it. Have you ever heard of anything so insane? I was punching a tree!"

Unintentionally, Ken sprang from his seat.

"Tree?"

"Yeah, a tree."

"A tree," Ken mumbled.

Slowly sitting back down, Ken recalled the story from the hospital, when the male nurse said Rhaymi drove into a tree on purpose.

"You didn't drive into a tree, did you?" Ken asked.

"No," Steph quickly answered. "But I would have. If there were a tree in front of me I would have plowed right into it. I was supposed to hit a guardrail, but instead I hit two construction barrels. And instead of driving into oncoming traffic, or a house, or a kid on a bike, or God knows what, I drove into a field and got stuck. And instead of running alone in the dark at night, a neighbor happened to find me. Looking back, I should have died that night, or at least been seriously hurt."

"On purpose or by accident?" Ken asked.

"Oh, either way. I didn't have control of what was going on, so anything could have happened."

Ken placed both of his hands behind his head and firmly began scratching. He looked at the three other group members, who all looked downward with hollow eyes.

"Can I ask you another question?" Ken asked before turning to Dr. Jonassen. "Doctor, can I ask Steph another question?"

"If it's OK with her."

Ken looked at the striking, confident woman.

"Go ahead, Buddy. What's your question?"

Ken placed his hands on his thighs. Then he lowered them below his knees before pulling them back as he sat upright in his chair.

"Why did you stay with him? Why did you stay with him for ... how long did you say?"

"Thirty-four years, since I was eighteen. We were married for twenty-nine years, after I got my MBA."

"Thirty-four years. Why did you stay with him for so long?"

"Because I loved him."

Steph's matter-of-fact and simple reply silenced the room again, and her stare locked onto Ken's eyes. Ken didn't flinch, fascinated by the answer.

"You loved him?"

"Yup. In a way, I still do."

"You still do?" answered Ken, his voice slightly raised.

"I know who my husband was. He was the funniest and kindest person I had ever met, and a complete gentleman. We had so much fun while we were dating and while we were engaged. He had so much energy; we did everything together. Florida, the Bahamas, Hawaii. We'd rent a Jeep and tool around on the beach at night. When he asked me to marry him, I didn't hesitate. He proposed to me on the beach; Key West. He knew I loved the beach."

"Yeah, but he started hurting you, and, what did you say, manipulating you?" Ken cautiously asked.

"Yup, he did. But even in the worst of times, I knew how wonderful of a person he could be. It was in there. I knew who he was."

"Are you still with him?" Ken asked.

"Nope, sixth time's a charm. It took my five-year-old niece to open my eyes."

"Your niece?" Ken said.

"Yeah. I had left my husband and was staying with my sister for a while, figuring I'd just go back again at some point. But one morning I was having breakfast and my niece asked me if I was tired. I said no and why was she asking. She said I never slept. I asked her what she meant by that and she said instead of sleeping at night, I cried.

"I knew I was doing it, but I never admitted it to myself. I cried every night. Every night for I don't know how many years, I cried at night."

Steph looked at everyone in the room, firm in her position.

"I got tired of crying every night. No one should have to cry every night. Fuck him."

"Where are you staying now?" Dr. Jonassen asked.

"Still with my sister. She has an extra room, and we get along well. Plus, her husband's a good guy – not an asshole. It's a good environment for me."

"Excellent," Dr. Jonassen replied. "You took a good first step – you surrounded yourself with a loving support group. That will give you the confidence you need to realize that it isn't you with the problem, that it was, in this case, your husband."

Steph nodded, and everyone else in the room followed.

"You have to understand something, and it's probably true in all of your cases," the doctor continued. "Long-term relationships typically don't start out rocky. Relationships that are rocky at the start don't last. People realize early that this isn't going to work out, and before the bond is too tight, someone leaves.

"But in most cases, like Steph's and Tracy's, and maybe yours," she said, looking at the young man, "long-term relationships start out great. There's fun, and excitement, and support, and love. Everything's wonderful. Trust is built, and you would do anything for your significant other. You've found your match."

Steph, sporting a half-smile, responded with a methodical nod.

"And then something happens," Dr. Jonassen continued. "But you think, 'no big deal.' And then it happens again, and you think, 'he or she must be having a bad day.' And then things keep happening, and you keep making excuses, because you know that's not how your significant other really is.

"After a time, when the bad moments start to roll into one another, you begin to question yourself. 'Is it me?' you wonder."

Pointing at the doctor, Steph looked at the wall as she repeated her nod.

"Well, when that happens day after day, week after week, month after month, year after year, you don't even know what to think anymore. It's called gaslighting."

Ken frowned. He had never heard of the term.

"It's common in abusive relationships. After all the lies, exaggerating and manipulating, you actually start to believe it when your significant other says things like 'you're worthless,' or 'this is all your fault,' or 'no one ... '"

"No one will ever want you," finished Steph. "Doc, don't forget, 'you're lucky to be with someone like me.' Yup, heard all of those a thousand times. At Christmas two years ago I got 'you don't deserve any presents.' That was a new one."

Ken rubbed his forehead with both of his hands.

"What did you call it? Gas ... ?"

"Gaslighting," answered the doctor. "Ultimately, the abuser, by any means possible, is trying to control the actions of the victim. Control; manipulation; coercion."

Ken adjusted himself in his seat, taking in the new information.

"Steph, you said something I think the group will find interesting," the doctor said. "You said you finally left your husband after six breakups, right?"

Steph nonchalantly nodded.

"In abusive relationships, it usually takes breaking up seven times before it finally sticks. That's the average."

"Seven?" Ken repeated.

"Seven," the doctor confirmed.

"You're kidding me?"

"No, unfortunately. Remember, it's gradual, with control and manipulation slowly entering; so slowly a person might not think anything of it at first. And then when it gets to be so bad, the victim is often so confused that they … "

" … drive their car into a tree," Ken finished softly.

"What's that?" asked the doctor.

"Nothing," Ken said, shaking his head.

"OK," the doctor said. "Well then, that's all the time we have for today. You all did wonderfully. That was an excellent discussion. Thank you for coming. Hopefully we will see all of you next Friday at four."

Popping up from his chair, Ken was the first to leave the room and the building, the bell on the door jingling as he walked briskly to his car. He unlocked the door, sat down, and pulled out his wallet, holding a business card close to his face. He leaned to his right, found his cell phone and dialed the number before placing the phone to his left ear as the ringer sounded.

"This is Dr. Harding," Ken heard, grimacing at hearing an answering machine. "I'm not in the office right now. Please leave your name and number and I will get back to you as soon as possible. If this is an emergency, please call nine, one, one."

Beeeeeeep.

"Hi, Doctor Harding," said Ken hurriedly. "This is Ken Roy. I used to volunteer at the hospital. I'm friends with a girl, Rhaymi

Summers. She was there a few weeks ago. You said for me to call you if there was ever a problem. Hey, I just got out of a group therapy session for abuse victims, and, um, I think Rhaymi's being abused by her boyfriend. Ahh, there's more to the story, but ... but I think she's being abused physically and emotionally. Ahh, if you want to know more, call me back. My cell phone number is 413-497-7111. Ken Roy; friends with Rhaymi Summers. Thank you, Doctor Harding."

After pushing a button, Ken leaned to his right again and put his phone in his pocket. He closed his eyes, took a deep breath, and released a long exhale. He stayed motionless for thirty seconds until he opened his eyes and looked into his rearview mirror.

"Fuck him."

Chapter 31

Click-clack-click-clack-click-clack.

The hooves perfectly repeated themselves along the pavement. The tuxedo-wearing rider proudly sat atop the lead horse of the parade, signifying the official start of the state fair.

"Hey, Celina, look at the horsey," Brooke said, leaning toward the front of the stroller as her daughter watched.

Two more horses with traditional-looking riders followed, ahead of a string of floats pulled by large pickup trucks. Ken had both hands on the handlebars of Celina's stroller as he blankly looked above the spectators on the other side of the parade. Brooke stood next to him.

"Daddy, are you tired?"

Ken shook his head, biting his bottom lip.

"You haven't said much. You usually really like the parade."

"I'm sorry, Sweetie. I've just got this whole thing with Rhaymi and her boyfriend and therapy and abuse and gaslighting on my mind."

"Gas what?"

"Gaslighting. Have you heard of it?"

"Haven't heard of that one."

"Well, I'm not sure I fully understand it either, but it's when someone in a relationship tries to have, for the most part, complete control over the other. They really just suck the life out of the other person, breaking them down emotionally. That's how I understand it, anyway."

"Oh, yeah, a controlling boyfriend is the worst. I had one of those once."

"Really?" Ken said, his full attention now on Brooke.

"Yeah. I didn't know how to handle it. It got to be pretty bad."

"When, in college or after college?"

"High school.

"In high school?" Ken blurted.

"Yeah."

"Who? Did I know him?"

"Of course you knew him, Daddy. It was Ricky Taylor."

"Ricky Taylor? The basketball player?"

"I only dated one Ricky Taylor."

Ken tugged hard at the lobe on his right ear, looking at the ground before peering back at Brooke.

"So, ahh, what happened?"

"He was just very controlling. He always wanted to know where I was and who I was with. He told me what to wear and what skirts were too short. And if he ever saw me talking to another boy at school, oh my God he would get so jealous. He'd tell me I didn't love him and ask how could I do that to him. It was exhausting."

"Really?"

"Yeah. Do you remember my prom, and how I came home early, and you asked why, and I said I was sick and must have gotten food poisoning?"

"Yeah."

"I had Jennifer drive me home before the prom was even over."

"Jennifer, our neighbor; your friend Jennifer?"

"Yeah."

"How come?"

"Well this boy, this sophomore boy who was at the prom with his sister, who I knew and was friends with, asked me to dance. Ricky wasn't around so I said sure. Well, as soon as that song was over, Ricky stormed onto the dance floor, grabbed me by the wrist and pulled me into the hallway."

"He grabbed your wrist?"

"That's not the worst of it. He was throwing this fit and at one point I rolled my eyes. When I did he grabbed me by my both of my shoulders and squeezed really hard."

Ken put his right hand on his forehead and ran it through his hair, strained by the story.

"I told him I was sick and ran to the bathroom. There was a girl I knew in there and she went and got Jennifer, and she gave me a ride home. I don't know what I would have done if she didn't have her car there."

Ken labored to process the story, his actions uneasy.

"Ricky Taylor grabbed you?"

"Yeah. I knew I should have broken up with him right there but I thought that would make things worse because he was so possessive. Thank God he cheated on me during the summer so I could break up with him."

"He cheated on you?"

"Yeah, with some girl you don't know. I could not *wait* to leave for Florida for college. I just needed to get out of here and get a fresh start."

Perplexed, Ken scratched the top of his head, processing the story as the parade participants marched by the onlookers.

"Did Mom know?"

"Nope."

"No? Well, why didn't you tell us?"

"That's not exactly something you go home and brag to your parents about. 'Hey, Mom and Dad, I'm dating a control freak. I'll be home at midnight,'" Brooke said with a fake smile.

"Come on; why didn't you tell us?"

"Tell you? Daddy, you and Mommy wouldn't have understood. You guys were like the Couple of the Century. Plus, you loved Ricky. You went to all of his basketball games, even the ones far away. You were always talking to him when he came over. You thought we were going to get married. You even said that you would be the best daycare center we could ever find."

Ken rubbed his forehead side-to-side, nodding in confirmation at Brooke's comments.

A large elephant, its face drooping and looking old, caught Ken's attention. Like a walking gray tank, the elephant lumbered step-by-step along the road as the parade goers cheered.

"So, how's James? Is he, um, has he ever … ?"

"James is a wonderful husband and father, Daddy. He doesn't have a bad bone in his body."

Ken let out a sigh and blinked hard twice.

"He tells me all the time we can move back up here if I want, but I could never do that to him. His dad is in such poor health, I could never make him leave. And he has a job he loves, and his younger brother lives next door with his wife, and they just had their first child. I couldn't pull him away from all of that, especially when he treats me like gold and I can fly up here whenever I want to see you."

"Yeah. He treats you like gold. You mean that?"

"Oh, yes, Daddy. He lets me do whatever I want."

"OK. Good."

A group of individuals dressed in suits concluded the parade. They all threw candy and waved to the spectators. Ken spotted Mayor Sullivan of Pynchonton, who walked with an open-mouthed smile. In a mental fog, Ken stared until the mayor walked past him.

"Daddy, are you OK?"

"Yeah, yeah. Um, so Sweetie, I'm sorry about Ricky."

"There's no need to apologize. You didn't know. Plus, Ricky was a charmer. He knew how to act around adults; he knew the game."

"The game?"

"Yeah. What do you expect, for him to start hollering at me and grabbing me in front of you? He knew how to put that big smile on every time he came over, laugh at all of your jokes, and rave about Mommy's food. It's just a game, Daddy; an act."

"An act?"

"Yeah, an act. You didn't see the real Ricky Taylor."

"But he was such a good basketball player, and you said he was a good student."

"Yeah, he was. But that doesn't mean he was a good boyfriend."

Ken slid both of his hands into his pockets and looked up at the nighttime sky. His eyes squinted.

"He works in Boston now, I think. I don't know. I haven't talked to him since I found out he cheated on me."

Ken closed his eyes and dropped his head, shaking it back-and-forth.

"Daddy, don't beat yourself up."

"I let you down. I let down my daughter; my own daughter."

"No, Daddy. You didn't let me down. You didn't know."

Ken turned, hearing a buzzing noise. Brooke quickly reached for her pocket and took out her cell phone.

"Hi, James."

Ken gave a small smile and then looked at Celina, who had a stuffed, fawn-colored pug next to her in her stroller.

"Oh my God. When?" Brooke said into her phone.

Concerned, Ken looked at Brooke.

"OK. I'll be there as soon as I can."

Ken raised his eyebrows.

"James, stop. I'll be home as soon as possible. I'll text you when I know my flight. Love you. Keep me posted."

Brooke shoved the phone in her front pocket and grabbed the stroller with both hands.

"I have to go back home, Daddy. James' dad fell off a ladder. Eighty years old, two bad knees, and he's on a ladder. Fell right on the cement driveway."

Brooke raced toward the exit, weaving in and out of the crowd. Ken followed, trotting in tow.

"Daddy, we have to go home to grab our things and then you have to take me to the airport. I know there's a nine o'clock flight to Orlando. Think we can make it?"

"We'll give it our best shot."

Chapter 32

Thump!

Ken grabbed the two suitcases off the pavement after closing the trunk.

"You can really book a flight on your phone?" Ken asked, looking to his right as he crossed the access road in front of the airport entrance.

"Of course, Daddy. Anyone can."

"I can't."

"Not with your phone you can't, but if you got a new phone you could."

"Really?"

"Yup, and a lot of other things. You just need an iPhone."

"Eyes phone?"

"Daddy? No, iPhone."

The glass double doors opened, and Brooke spotted the counter for her airline. She zigzagged her way through the sectioned-off area before stepping to the attendant. After showing her driver's license, she grabbed her boarding pass, shoved it in her front pocket and raced toward the security gate with both hands tightly on the blue handlebars of Celina's stroller.

"OK, Daddy. Sorry, but I have to go." Brooke said, leaning toward Celina. "Say bye to Grampy."

Ken bent over and kissed his granddaughter. Her head was already turned to the right, making her left cheek an easy target. He and Brooke gave each other a quick kiss on the lips.

"Bye, Daddy. Love you."

"Love you, Sweetie. Bye. Bye, bye, Celina," he said, waving his right hand up and down, thoroughly bending his wrist. In no time, Brooke and Celina were through the security line and out of sight, twenty minutes before their unexpected flight was scheduled to depart.

Ken drove home, thinking of his daughter and granddaughter, hoping their flight home went as planned and wondering when he would see them again. When he arrived home, he rested the keys on the kitchen counter and walked directly to his recliner. He plopped himself down and let out a long sigh; his last ten hours had been at a hurried pace. He could feel his body calming down, quickly shifting to a feeling of exhaustion. His back began to melt into his familiar seat, and his breathing became deeper and deeper.

Without a fight, his eyes closed, but only for a second. He reached into his left pocket, feeling the buzz of his phone. He opened it without looking at the number.

"Hello."

He heard breathing on the other end. It was ragged; up-and-down.

"Hello?" he repeated, slightly sitting up.

"I think ... he's ... he's ... he's going ... to ... to kill me."

Ken sprang from his chair.

"Rhay? Rhaymi, is that you?"

With faint yelling in the background, the stressed breathing increased for a moment before Ken heard a ring tone on the other end.

"Hello? Hello?"

Ken pushed a button and looked at the number. It was Rhaymi's cell number. He carefully pushed all 10 digits. The phone rang four times before there was an answer.

"Hey, hey, hey. This is Rhay. Leave a message and I'll call you back later – todaaaaay."

Beep.

"Rhaymi, answer your phone. Answer your phone, or, or, call me back."

Ken closed the top of his flip-phone, sprinted up the stairs, came down in a minute, grabbed the keys off the counter and raced out the door.

Chapter 33

The silver Toyota Camry absorbed the shock from the speed bumps. Ken was surprised there was no security guard in the shack at the entrance of the campus since it was nighttime on a Friday. He craned his neck, searching for something familiar. He'd never been at Pynchonton College at night before. He swerved to his left to avoid a group of oncoming students walking in the road.

"Come on. Come on," he whispered, searching for anything he recognized.

"There," he continued, his voice raising as he spotted the bronze statue of Jesus Christ.

Recognizing the place he had dropped off Rhaymi, he accelerated and soon saw what he believed was her dorm. He pulled the car over to the right and got out, ignoring the red and white "Tow Zone" sign on the metal pole. He jogged to the dorm and, after two girls entered the building, he lunged forward, grabbing the brass handle before the door closed.

"Excuse me?" Ken said, his right hand in the air.

The girls turned around. Their eyes were bloodshot, and they wore looks of disgust on their tired faces.

Unfazed, Ken asked, "Do you know where Rhaymi lives? Rhaymi, ahh, Summers?"

"That way," one of the girls said as she nonchalantly pointed to her right toward a wooden door. The girls kept walking as Ken whipped the door open, revealing a long hallway.

"Oh geez."

Once inside, though, Ken saw small whiteboards attached to the doors; most displayed names of who lived in each room.

He briskly walked down the hall, looking from the right side of the hall to the left as he moved.

"Joan and Susan; Mae-Day and Aman-Day; Hannah and Joyfulness; Susan and Fra-Fra-Fra-Frances; Margie and Peg; Thunder and Uno Queen of the World. Ken froze, staring at the whiteboard for room number 125. He looked to his right and left before looking back at the door and taking a step closer. He could hear something. A door behind him opened, causing Ken to flinch.

"Can I help you, Sir?" asked a girl dressed in dark jeans and a flannel blue and gray shirt.

"What?" Ken responded, still slightly startled.

"Can I help you? I'm the R.A. Are you someone's parent?"

"No, I'm Rhaymi's friend. R.A.? What does that mean?"

"Resident assistant. I'm in charge of the floor, Sir."

"You're in charge? Open the door. Rhaymi called me earlier. She's in trouble. I think she's in her room being abused by her boyfriend. Open the door; open the door right now."

The R.A. dashed into her room and grabbed a lanyard off her desk, the pile of keys jingling as she sprinted to the door. She sifted through one key after another before stopping, putting it in the keyhole and turning the knob, hitting the lights as she burst into the room with Ken a step behind her.

"What the hell?!" came a yell from a bed in the left corner. A girl with short black hair looked at the R.A. and Ken, as a boy pulled a maroon comforter over their naked bodies.

"Jules, what are you doing in my room?" the girl said, Ken turning away. "Get out!"

Jules turned and quickly exited, giving Ken a nudge on her way before closing the door.

"Mister, I'm going to get in big trouble," the R.A. snapped as Ken looked at the tan carpeted floor.

"I ... "

The door to the room flung open. It was the girl, wrapped in the maroon comforter.

"Jules, what on earth were you thinking? It's Friday night. I have the room to myself Friday nights. You know that."

"I know. I'm sorry. I forgot."

"You forgot? How can you forget? It's been that way all year."

"I know. I know. This guy knocked on my door and said Rhaymi was in trouble and he told me to open the door."

"Rhaymi? She's not even here."

"Rhaymi isn't here?" Ken responded.

"Noooo! She left this afternoon with her boyfriend; said she was going to some group thing; therapy thing. I don't know; something like that."

Ken's eyes opened, his heart pounded, and his stomach dropped. He turned and ran down the hallway, not slowing down as he slammed hands first through the wooden door and then through the door to the outside, arms pumping and his knees high as he sprinted toward his car. He got inside and closed the door. Then he closed his eyes and kept them closed.

"Heapstown; golf course; dead end street; white Corvette," he said.

Starting the car and pulling away in one motion, Ken cut the wheel hard to the left, jumping the curb and bouncing back into the road. With the entrance gate soon in sight, his tire barely bounced as he sped over the speed bumps as he raced away from the college.

Chapter 34

The moon gave off enough light to brighten the Heapstown Country Club on the right. Ken let off the gas pedal, knowing there was a road nearby. A green sign with white letters read "Birdie Lane." He slowed and turned right. His heart raced, and his head twisted from side-to-side. He wasn't sure what he was looking for, or even if he was on the right street.

The Camry crawled along the road, which was filled with massive homes surrounded by trees and shrubs. The cul-de-sac neared, circling Ken to the right toward the last house. He slowed even more. He saw a parked car pulled closely to the garage, partly camouflaged by chest-high bushes. He stopped, craning his neck to try to get a better look. He cut his wheel to the right and cautiously entered the driveway. His tires gradually rolled forward: five feet, ten feet, twenty feet. He pushed down on the brake.

"White Corvette," he whispered.

Turning off his lights and shutting off the car, he got out and quietly closed the door. He walked deliberately to the front door, pushing up slightly onto his tiptoes with his head jutted forward. He stopped at the bottom of the single step, frowning and cocking his head. He could hear something. His eyes moved, trying to decipher the intermittent sounds. He stepped up onto the cement platform, stopping again to listen.

"What is that?" he muttered.

Another step put him inches from the door, where the porch was well-lit by a single light. He turned his ear to the door, the furrowing of his eyebrows the only movement he made. He heard a deep voice coming from inside. It was loud. Ken stood upright, realizing he only heard one voice. He couldn't determine whether it was the TV or a person shouting. As he continued to stand still, his ears adjusted, and he could pick out words and phrases, but still in just one voice.

"Waste of my time!" Ken heard clearly. He leaned even closer, with his ear touching the door. The voice lowered, but he could still hear something. Then it spiked again.

"I can't believe you did that!"

Ken still wasn't sure what he was hearing. He pressed his fingertips gently against the metal door. He closed his eyes and took deep breaths, trying to remain patient.

"I will throw this cat out the fucking window!"

"Cat?" Ken questioned as his head shot up.

He leaned back toward the door.

"Stupid fucking cat!"

"Please, no."

It was the first time he had heard a second voice – a crying voice. He grabbed the shiny brass knob with his left hand and twisted his wrist. It wasn't locked. He carefully pushed, and the door opened with ease.

"You have no idea how much I hate this fucking cat!"

For the first time, the voices weren't muffled, and he could tell the sound wasn't coming from a television. It came from a person – an angry person.

"Please, Mathew, no. Please don't hurt Freddie," a voice whimpered in return.

"Shut up. It's my house. You'll do and say what I tell you to do and say in my house. It's my house. Mine. You should feel lucky I even let you stay here."

The argument was clearly coming from his left. Ken slowly stepped in that direction, toward an open interior doorframe.

"Do you want to stay here this summer? Do you?"

Ken heard the sound of sobbing follow the yelling.

"If you want to stay here you have to do what I say!"

"Please don't hurt Freddie," the crying voice begged.

"Shut the fuck up about the fucking cat!"

"Please," a whining voice pleaded.

"That's it! I'm killing the fucking thing!"

Ken was a step away from the doorframe. He saw Rhaymi on the floor to his right, sitting on the back of her calves. Her face was full of tears, and her hair was tangled. Ken stepped into the doorframe and saw Mathew holding the handle of the cat carrier in his right hand, at eye level.

"I'm going to throw him out the fucking window if you don't shut the fuck up!" Mathew raged. "I'm going to throw the cat out the fucking window, and then I'm going to throw *you* out the fucking window!"

Ken grabbed the bottom of his shirt with his left hand and lifted it up a few inches.

"Please, stop, Mathew," Rhaymi cried. "Please."

"You're telling me what to do in my house? That's it, I'm killing the fucking cat!"

"That's enough."

Rhaymi's crying stopped immediately, and Mathew lowered the cat carrier to his waist. They both looked toward the figure in the doorframe.

Ken stood just as he had talked – calmly. A black pistol was in his right hand, and his left foot and shoulder were thrust forward. The stubbed barrel was pointed directly at the homeowner.

"Put Freddie down," he said in a soothing voice.

Rhaymi stared at Ken, who remained motionless, framed by the doorway's white trim. His determined eyes stayed fixed on Rhaymi's boyfriend.

"Get the fuck out of my house, guy," said Mathew, his voice shifting from rage to disgust.

Slowly, Ken responded, "Give ... the cat ... to Rhaymi."

After pausing, Mathew walked toward Rhaymi, the men's eyes locked on one another. Rhaymi, her face desperate, reached for the crate. Mathew looked at Rhaymi, his eyes cold, and lifted the cat carrier out of her reach. He turned to Ken.

"Make me."

Ken squeezed his right index finger.

BANG!

Ken's shot came without hesitation, expression, or movement. The single blast went into a wall, intentionally to the left of Mathew, who ducked down at the sound of the explosion. Rhaymi's face changed from fear to amazement, her eyes wide open and her hands still extended.

The echo of the shot lessened, and silence fell upon the room.

"The next one doesn't miss," said Ken, keeping his mild demeanor. "Give Freddie to Rhay."

Mathew lowered the cat carrier to Rhaymi, who clutched the plastic box and pulled it closely to her body while looking at her stunned boyfriend.

"Time to go, Rhay."

Rhaymi slid back out of Mathew's reach and stood, wrapping her arms around the carrier. She looked at Ken, then at her boyfriend, took two steps, and looked back again at Mathew as she walked through the doorframe.

"Sorry," she whispered as Ken stepped aside.

Ken maintained his gaze on Mathew, whose eyes darted throughout the room.

"Stay away from Rhay."

Mathew didn't move. Ken walked slowly backward in a straight line, keeping the pistol's aim on Mathew, who got smaller and smaller in the doorframe. Rhaymi stood anxiously at the door. Ken grabbed the knob without looking and opened it, moving forward to let Rhaymi step outside behind him.

With the front door open, Ken kept the pistol pointed at Mathew. He waited a few seconds and then a few more. He stepped outside and lowered his gun but only after repeating:

"Stay away from Rhay."

Chapter 35

Ken looked in his rearview mirror as he drove away from the house on Birdie Lane, half expecting Mathew to follow him. When he turned left onto the main road toward Pynchonton, his concerns subsided, allowing him the opportunity to give Rhaymi his full attention.

"You OK?"

"Yeah."

"You sure? Are you hurt?"

"No, I'm OK."

"OK, good. Freddie all right?"

Rhaymi picked up the carrier and looked at Freddie through the slots on the side.

"I think so. He was in his crate the whole time."

Ken nodded and his body started to relax, knowing Rhaymi wasn't hurt.

"Can I ask you a question, Rhay? Why didn't you go to the group therapy?"

"I was planning to," she answered, still looking at Freddie. "Mathew texted me right after you called, and I asked him if he could give me a ride. He said he would. When he picked me up he told me to get Freddie because he had some leftover fish for him. He knows how much Freddie loves fish.

"The ride was great. We were laughing and singing to his playlist. I told him to just forget about the therapy because we were having so much fun. I didn't want to ruin it."

Ken shook his head, seeing the various ways Mathew had manipulated Rhaymi.

"When we got to his house he asked me why I didn't return his text. I told him I really didn't want to talk about it. He said he loved me and was worried about me. I told him I just wanted to focus on my finals. Well, he didn't like that, and that's when he grabbed me."

"He grabbed you?"

"Yeah."

"Why didn't you just leave?"

"Well, I knew that would upset him."

"Upset him? Rhay, he grabbed you."

"Yeah, but it was just by my shirt. It didn't hurt."

Ken shook his head slightly, but not enough for Rhaymi to notice.

"Plus, it's my fault he was mad. I didn't let him know where I was all week. He was concerned about me. He loves me. I should have replied to his text."

"When did he text you?"

"Friday during his lunch break."

"Friday? But you did text him Friday. You said he texted you and you replied and asked for a ride."

"Yeah, but I didn't text him back right away. When Mathew texts, he likes a reply right away."

The more Rhaymi talked, the more Ken connected the dots. He let Rhaymi finish talking, not saying anything until there was a pause in the conversation.

"Rhay, you really think this guy loves you?"

"Of course he loves me. He tells me all the time he loves me. And he shows me, too. He buys me lots of things. He's paid for almost all of my clothes, and we've traveled all over the place. I never have to pay for anything when we go out or when we go to his summer place."

Again, Ken waited before replying, hoping Rhaymi would hear her own words.

"Rhay, you really think this guy loves you?"

"Of course he does."

"Well, Rhay, love is a tricky word. Anyone can say they love someone else. And money, well, money can cover up a lot of things."

For the first time, Rhaymi took her eyes off Freddie and looked at Ken.

"Here, I'm going to ask you a different question: do you think you're in a healthy relationship?"

Rhaymi turned her attention back to Freddie, sticking her fingers into one of the slots. Freddie responded with a gentle tap of his paw in return.

"He loves me," Rhaymi answered in a deadpan tone.

"That's not what I asked you. I asked you if you think you're in a healthy relationship."

"He just gets mad sometimes. It's usually my fault. I usually do something that sets him off. I say some pretty stupid things."

"Rhay, I was married forty-five years. Over that time, my wife said some things I didn't always agree with, or things I really didn't like."

Rhaymi looked back at Ken, who took his eyes off the road to make his point.

"I never hit her."

Rhaymi looked away, and Ken did the same while continuing his statement.

"I never grabbed her, I never yelled at her, and I never swore at her. And I certainly never threatened to throw her out of a window."

"He didn't mean that."

"Oh, I'd disagree. That was an angry, dangerous person, Rhay. You deserve better than that; so much better."

Ken looked in his rearview mirror, noticing a car quickly catching up to him. He thought about speeding up, but he didn't. Within seconds the car was right behind him. Ken was relieved to see it wasn't Mathew's Corvette, but instead a police car. Ken looked back toward the road. The cruiser's lights came on. Ken frowned, wondering what he had done. Ken saw a good spot to pull over fifty feet ahead, waited, and veered to the right. He stopped the car, rolled down his window, and put both of his hands on the steering wheel.

An officer exited his cruiser, and Ken saw another police car with its lights on approaching from ahead of him, already crossing the double line and speeding directly for Ken's car.

"License and registration, please," said the young Pynchonton officer, whose broad shoulders and short hair fit the stereotypical description of a cop.

"What seems to be the problem, Officer?"

"Out of the car, Sir," the officer responded, opening Ken's door and stepping to the side.

Ken hesitated, still uncertain of what was unfolding. He slowly twisted, placing his feet on the pavement. He hesitated again before standing.

"Hands against the car, please."

Ken frowned. Even though he had never been pulled over, he knew this was not proper protocol.

"Hands against the car, please," the officer sternly repeated.

As instructed, Ken turned around and placed both of his hands above the window of his car. The officer reached for Ken's mid-section, pulling up his shirt and grabbing the small gun in Ken's waistband. The officer grabbed Ken's right wrist, and in three movements, his hands were handcuffed behind his back.

"What's going on?" Ken pleaded.

The other officer walked directly to Ken and grabbed him under his right armpit and lifted. The first officer did the same to his left armpit, while grasping the back of the collar on Ken's shirt and pulling him away from his car.

"Rhay, drive to your dorm and stay there. Don't go anywhere," Ken instructed.

"This way, Sir," the first officer said. He marched Ken to the cruiser before opening the back door, lowering his head, and putting him into the back of the car.

Chapter 36

Slam. Click.

The metal door to the holding cell closed, and Ken heard the sound of the officer turning the lock.

"Can you tell me why I'm in here?"

The officer didn't reply, just like all of the other officers Ken had crossed paths with since being arrested. Something caught Ken's attention. He curled his nose, turned around and saw two other people in the cell. His nose wrinkled even more; and the smell made his eyes squint. He looked into the back right corner, where he noticed green liquid with chunks mixed in it on the floor. A man, wearing at least three coats, slept on the floor.

Another man, bald, with tattoos covering his neck and running up the back of his head, stood facing the left wall. Ken sat on a metal bench on the right, his left hand brushing against the metal bars. He could see a clock in the hallway. It read 12:04.

Throughout the night, various officers walked by the holding cell. Ken asked each the same question: "Can I talk to the person in charge, please?"

None of the officers replied. Hour after hour passed. The man staring at the wall was taken out, but the drunk stayed, hardly moving during the night. Ken never became tired. He was wired by the night's events, and his rush to the airport felt like a lifetime ago.

Ken heard footsteps. He looked up and saw an officer walking toward him. Ken stood and stepped forward, meeting the young cop at the other end of the cell.

"Officer, I haven't been able to make a phone call. That's against my rights as a citizen."

"We're still processing your paperwork, Sir," said the officer, not breaking stride.

Ken walked side-by-side with the officer before running out of room in the cell. He sat back down, in the same spot as before.

"Paperwork?"

Ken knew something was wrong all along, but he couldn't put his finger on exactly what. An officer he hadn't seen all night told him there was a problem with his paperwork. Not only had Ken not done any paperwork, but why would this officer know there was a problem if he had? He sat, trying to piece together the situation. Another hour passed before Ken realized

something in the silence of his cell that made his head shoot up.

"Captain O'Donnell."

Chapter 37

Clump, clump, clump, clump.

The footsteps echoed in the hallway outside the holding

cell, where Ken stood behind the bars of the door. He stopped

asking questions, knowing it wasn't going to do any good, and

believing he was going to be paid a visit by a certain officer. That

officer appeared at 7:17 a.m.

Captain Francis "Frank" O'Donnell appeared to Ken's

right. Carrying a clipboard, he wore a white cap on top of his

buzz cut. His barrel chest, combined with his height, made him

an imposing physical figure.

"Ken Roy," the captain said, his baritone voice thundering

throughout the cinderblock walls.

Ken confidently nodded, keeping his gaze on the officer.

"Looks like you got yourself into a little bit of a pickle

here, Mr. Roy. Attempted murder, illegally discharging a firearm, breaking and entering, kidnapping, speeding, failure to stop for an officer, resisting arrest, unlawfully carrying a firearm. That's a pretty big laundry list."

Unfazed, Ken maintained his look upon the captain. The captain flipped through the multiple papers on the clipboard.

"Biiiiiig laundry list," repeated the captain. "Anything to say for yourself, Mr. Roy?"

"I'd like to make a phone call."

"You'd like to make a phone call?"

"Yes, Captain. I'm allowed one phone call."

The captain chuckled before replying, "That's true, Mr. Roy. You are allowed one phone call, and you've already made it."

Ken frowned, knowing he did not make a phone call since he had arrived.

"See, right here."

The captain turned the clipboard toward Ken and pointed to a line near the bottom.

"You called this number at 1:12 in the morning. I believe that's your home number. We have it documented that someone answered. I don't know who answered; we don't keep track of that, but we do have in your file that someone did answer. Therefore, Mr. Roy, you have been granted your one phone call, and you will not be granted anymore."

The captain gave Ken a smirk, turned, and walked back in the direction he had come. Ken's confidence was gone. He sat in the same place he had been most of the night. He recognized he was in trouble, and he needed to think of something. What that something was, though, he had no idea.

Chapter 38

All morning and all afternoon, shady-looking men came into the cell, had their names called an hour or two later, and never came back. Ken, though, was going on sixteen hours. He hadn't eaten, and he hadn't slept. He originally thought about trying to run when the cell door opened to let someone out, but he knew that would just make matters worse. He figured he was going to get released when the captain decided, or if he could figure out a way to make a phone call.

Clump, clump, clump, clump. Officers regularly walked by the cell, not paying attention to anyone inside. Ken always looked up, looking for any sign of hope.

The black and white analog clock read 4:16 in the afternoon. Footsteps rang throughout the hallway, and Ken looked up, just as he had done a hundred times already. Ken stared as a thirty-something-year-old officer walked by the vertical bars of the cell, his eyes straight ahead.

"Ricky?"

The officer turned while walking two more steps.

"Ricky Taylor?" Ken asked as he stood, wrapping his hands around the bars.

"Mr. Roy?" came the reply. The officer stopped his stride with a perplexed look.

"Hey, Ricky. How are you?" asked Ken, his tone somewhat excited.

"Mr. Roy, it's great to see you."

"Great to see you, too. I thought you were out in Boston?"

"Yeah, I was, but I was stuck on third shift. I heard there was a second shift opening here, applied, and got the job. I started last week."

"Well, welcome back. Welcome back. It's funny, Brooke and I were just talking about you yesterday."

"Yeah? How's she doing?"

"Great. Living in Florida, teaching at a college. She's married and had her first child a few months ago."

"That's great to hear."

"Yeah. She married a good guy; he's good to her. But I'll be honest, you were my favorite, Ricky. I loved going to your basketball games and watching you play. You were a great player; real heady."

"Well, I don't know about great, but I loved it."

"Oh, and it showed, Ricky. It showed."

Ricky briefly scratched the back of his head.

"Mr. Roy, what are you doing in here? You're about as perfect as a person can be."

Ken looked down, bending his right knee and tapping the toe of his sneaker on the cement.

"Well, Ricky, I've got some bad news. I could use a little help.'

"Anything for you, Mr. Roy. You always treated me like, well .. I always felt really comfortable at your house."

"Thanks, Ricky, and I always enjoyed having you around. So, here's the deal."

Stepping back from the bars, Ken placed his hands in front of his waist and closed his eyes.

"I'm an alcoholic."

"What?! You?!"

"Yeah," Ken continued, opening his eyes. "I don't know if you heard or not, but my wife died a few months ago, and my best friend, Mr. Huber, died a few months before that. When I retired I just got bored and started drinking."

"Really? You, Mr. Roy?"

"Yeah. It started out harmless enough - a couple drinks while I was watching the Sox or Bruins or Celtics at night. But then I started going out, driving around to different bars."

"I don't believe you."

Ken hesitated for what felt like a lifetime, not knowing if Ricky meant what he said literally or just as a figure of speech.

"I know, I know. I never drank, but it's funny what being alone can do to you," said Ken, looking into the officer's eyes.

Ricky paused before replying, "Geez, Mr. Roy. I'm so sorry to hear that."

"And so last night, I went out. I can't even remember where, and I got pulled over for drinking and driving. Thank God the Pynchonton police pulled me over. I could have killed somebody. I woke up just a few minutes ago. I don't even know what time it is."

Ricky took out his cell phone and looked at the screen.

"It's 4:20."

"In the afternoon?! What a helpless sap I am. I've been in here for who knows how many hours. I haven't even made my phone call."

"You haven't made your phone call?"

Ken shook his head, looking down where the bars meet the floor.

"Oh, well, Mr. Roy, let's take care of that. You want to make your call. Here, let me unlock the door. Let me just go to the officer in charge and I'll get the key."

"Oh, Ricky, I'd rather you didn't. I'm … I'm afraid I might see someone I know. I'm really embarrassed. I'm embarrassed just talking to you."

"Don't be embarrassed. Alcohol can be so addicting. My dad …"

The officer stopped, dropping his head as he held the phone between his thumb and index finger.

"Yeah, Ricky, I know."

The stunned officer kept his gaze toward the concrete floor.

"Hey, Ricky," Ken continued. "Can I just grab your phone to call my neighbor? You know my neighbor, Mr. Flanagan?"

"Jennifer's dad? From the newspaper?"

"Yeah. I just want to tell him to, ahh, let my dog out. Poor thing's been inside all morning and afternoon. Looks like I'll have a present waiting for me on the rug when I get home."

Ricky paused, continuing to move his phone up and down. Ken's heart pounded, and he worked to keep his composure.

"Sure, Mr. Roy. Here you go," Ricky said, tapping the screen and typing in the code to unlock the phone.

"Thanks, Ricky. You have no idea how much I appreciate this."

"No problem."

"Hey, Ricky," Ken continued, taking a step back, "I'm just going to back up, for a little privacy. This ... this is all so embarrassing."

"No problem," answered Ricky, putting his palms up at shoulder level. "I understand. Here, I'll step out of sight."

"Oh, Ricky. What a great officer. You're so understanding."

Ken tapped the screen, turned, and walked to the back of the cell.

"Please be home, please be home," Ken mumbled.

"Hello?"

"Robbie! Oh, thank God you answered."

"Ken?"

"Yeah."

"Is something the matter?"

"Yeah, I'm in jail."

"What?"

"I'm in jail."

"Why?"

"Long story. Robbie, I need you to do two things for me. First, you have Mayor Sullivan's number, right?"

"What?"

"You have Mayor Sullivan's number?"

"Well, yeah, of course I do."

"OK. Call the mayor and tell him you're running a front page story on a corrupt cop in tomorrow's Sunday newspaper."

"Front page story? We don't have a front page story on a corrupt cop."

"I know, I know. But … Robbie, do you want to see me again?"

"See you again? Ken, what the hell are you talking about?"

"Robbie, if you want to see me again, call the mayor, tell him you are running a front page story on a corrupt cop … no, no … a corrupt captain. OK? Can you do that, right now?"

"You're serious?"

"Robbie, I'm in jail, and I'm looking at being in jail the rest of my life if you don't do this for me."

"OK, I'll call him right now," Robbie agreed.

"Great, thanks."

"Ken?"

"What?"

"What's the other thing?"

"What?"

"The other thing. You said you needed me to do two things for you."

"Oh, that's right. Come get me out of jail."

Chapter 39

A metal door from the left side of the cell opened in a manner Ken hadn't heard in his seventeen hours in the cell. A fast-paced *clump-clump-clump-clump* became louder. Standing with conviction at the cell's door, Ken looked at the clock, which read 4:51 p.m.

"You picked the wrong guy to mess with, Roy."

Captain O'Donnell's face was red, and he walked with rage in his eyes as he pointed at Ken.

"Corrupt cop? You ain't seen nothin', buddy." I will let you rot ... "

"Frankie," calmly said Commissioner Thomas Jenkins, who strolled behind the captain. "Take it easy."

"Yeah, Francis. Take it easy," said Ken, his chin up and his chest out.

"You wanna get cute, tough guy? OK, we'll see how cute you are when you get tagged with twenty years for attempted murder – attempted murder against my son!"

"Maybe your son will be my cell mate."

"Why, you motherfucker," said the captain as he lunged forward and reached between the bars.

Ken caught the captain's right arm with both hands and pushed it as hard as he could to the left, into the bars and away from the captain's body, sending the big man into an equally large scream.

"Mr. Roy, let go of Captain O'Donnell," Commissioner Jenkins said sternly.

Ken, looking at the commissioner, let go immediately and stepped back, regaining his stance behind the metal bars.

"Ken!"

Turning to his left, Ken saw Robbie walking side-by-side with Mayor Sullivan.

"What the hell is going on here," demanded the stocky mayor, his round face beat red. "Why am I getting a phone call from Rob on a Saturday afternoon about a corrupt captain, presumably you, Captain O'Donnell? Can someone please answer that question for me?"

"Oh, I'll gladly answer that. Robbie already knows the story because I told him earlier, but I'll fill you in."

Robbie was confused but maintained a poker face.

"So, long story short, I've become friends with a girl at Pyncnonton College, and she happens to be dating Captain O'Donnell's son."

"How did you become friends with her anyway?" the captain snidely asked. "Are you some pervert, going after girls forty years younger than you?"

"Great segue, Captain. Thank you," Ken replied sarcastically. "I was volunteering at the hospital when I met Rhaymi. In just a two-month span she was admitted to the hospital four times. Four times! After the last time, a counselor – a professional psychologist - said she thought Rhaymi was being abused. Now, remember, I didn't say that - a professional psychologist said that.

"Well, one day I fell when I was running in the park and Rhaymi happened to be there. She drove me home because I couldn't see. She patched me up, then we ran a marathon together a few weeks later, and we became friends.

"So, I came to find out that your son," said Ken, pointing firmly at the captain, "has been manipulating and coercing and kicking the crap out of this girl for God knows how long."

The Captain dropped his head and licked his lips as he looked from the Mayor to the Commissioner and then back to Ken.

"So, I got Rhaymi to agree to go to a group therapy session for victims of abuse with me on Friday. I couldn't take her because my daughter's flight got in late, so Rhaymi called your zipperhead son. But instead of taking her to the support group, the dip-shit tricked her and took her back to his place, where he threatened to throw her out a window."

Ken lifted his hands away from his side, and placed them head high.

"I heard that with my own ears – that guy's son said he was going to throw someone out a window. So did I go into someone's house when technically I wasn't supposed to? Yes. And did I fire off a shot inside a house? Yes, I did.

"And you should be happy I did, Captain," continued Ken, his entire attention now on the man directly in front of him. "Because if I wasn't there, your son would be behind these bars for murder. Or would you have pulled a few strings and made sure that didn't happen?"

The fury returned to Captain O'Donnell's eyes as he stepped forward and clutched both bars.

"You watch what you say," he seethed.

Ken stepped forward, a slight smile crossing his face.

"Hey, Captain. Watch this."

Ken took one step to his left so he could bypass the Captain.

"Mr. Commissioner, have you changed your phone call policy?"

"Excuse me?"

"Have you changed your phone call policy? I was never granted a phone call."

"But you said you called Rob."

"Oh, I did, but that was after I tricked one of your new officers into letting me borrow his phone. That was a little after four this afternoon. I came in around midnight. I went 16 hours without being granted a phone call. And the best part is Captain Ding-Dong here has paperwork saying I did. What the Captain is failing to recognize, and which surprises me, given his experience, is that I would have made that call in a room where I'm sure there's a security camera, and I'm one hundred percent certain that security camera will reveal that I never made a phone call."

Still hanging onto the bars, Captain O'Donnell looked down and shook his head.

"I haven't eaten either – not a bite of food or drink of water in, how long has it been now, seventeen hours?"

"This man hasn't had anything to eat or drink in seventeen hours?" barked the Mayor. "Thomas, how can that happen? This isn't the Wild West. What the hell are you thinking?"

'Oh, Mr. Mayor, I'm saving the best for last for the Commissioner. He's going to love this one."

The Mayor and Captain looked at the Commissioner, whose face grew concerned.

"Mr. Commissioner, you might be interested in knowing that when I was pulled over last night by two of your officers," Ken said as his eyes panned the three men, "I wasn't read my Miranda Rights."

The three men stood with their mouths open. The Mayor put his hands on his head, the Commissioner rubbed his forehead, and the Captain dropped his head in disgust. Ken kept his eyes on the Commissioner.

"Mr. Roy, are you one hundred percent certain that you were not read your rights when you were pulled over last night?" the Commissioner asked.

'Yes, Mr. Commissioner," Ken instantly replied. "I'm sure."

"And Robbie, can you vouch for Mr. Roy's character?" the Commissioner probed. "Is he a good citizen of our community?"

"I've known Ken for most of my life. He's as clean as they come, Mr. Commissioner."

The Commissioner stuck his right hand into his pocket, stepped forward, lightly tapped the Captain on the right shoulder with the back of his left hand, unlocked the cell, and opened the door.

"Thank you, Mr. Commissioner," said Ken as he walked through the opening.

After a brief pause, Ken stepped toward the Captain.

"This is the first thing you're going to do," said Ken, his chin inches away from the Captain. "Your son is beating on a nineteen-year-old girl. I know it, he knows it, and you know it. That has to stop – *now*."

Ken paused, waiting for some sort or reaction from the Captain.

"Frank, is this true? Has Mathew been abusing someone?" the Commissioner asked.

The Captain looked down and then looked at the Commissioner.

"He probably could have handled a couple situations better," answered the Captain, as the Mayor and Commissioner rolled their eyes and took deep breaths. "OK, I'll get him to some counseling."

"Good. And now, Mr. Commissioner," continued Ken, taking a step away from the Captain. "I need you to watch the Captain make that appointment with a counselor and make sure he follows through on those appointments. A nineteen-year-old girl dating the son of one of your captains was nearly thrown out a window last night."

"The appointments will get taken care of, Mr. Roy."

"Thank you. Now, gentlemen, let's get one thing straight – all of the charges against me are going to be dropped. If you do not do that, Robbie Flanagan, my neighbor of forty-plus years, is going to run a story on the cover of the newspaper – *his* newspaper - and that story will get you fired," said Ken, pointing at the Captain, "you fired," he continued, pointing at the Commissioner, "and you will not be re-elected," he finished, pointing at the Mayor.

Crossing his arms, Ken stood firmly in front of the four most powerful men in the city of Pynchonton.

"The public tends to look down upon those involved in corruption cases, especially corruption cases involving police departments."

Ken stepped toward the exit. Robbie turned to walk by his side, giving his neighbor two firm pats on the back.

"And one last thing, gentlemen. If anything should *happen to me*," said Ken, using air quotes, "remember, the editor-in-chief of the region's biggest newspaper knows everything."

Chapter 40

Tick-tick; tick-tick; tick-tick.

Robbie waited to turn left out of the parking lot at the Pynchonton Police Station. Ken sat in the front passenger seat of the SUV staring straight ahead.

"I gotta tell ya, Ken, that surprised me in there. You were a little out of character," Robbie said, pulling into the road.

"Only a little?"

"Yeah, right. More than a little; a lot. I don't think I've ever seen you act like that."

Ken slightly nodded his head, maintaining his stony gaze.

"You usually take orders, Ken. You do what your told, and without complaint or attention. But in there, boy, you were in charge."

"Didn't think I had it in me?"

"Well, no, because I've been neighbors with you for forty-something years and I've never seen you remotely act like that. Jesus Ken, you were telling a police captain, the police commissioner, and the Mayor how to do their jobs. People don't talk to them like that."

"Well, maybe people should."

"And you lied, Ken, telling them we had a front-page story. Have you ever lied before?"

"Never; not until the last few days. Had to."

"That's so out of character. That's not like you at all. What's gotten into you? You're one of the nicest, kindest people I know, and now you're getting thrown in jail and lying to the police and the Mayor."

"You left out shooting guns."

"What?"

"Shooting guns. I shot a gun – sent a bullet right over a kid's head last night."

"What?!"

"He said he was going to throw Rhaymi out the window."

"I didn't know you owned a gun."

"Well," Ken said, tapping Robbie on the shoulder with the back of his left hand, "that's not something you go blabbing to the neighbors about."

"Yeah, I suppose not."

Both men kept their eyes on the sign for Riversville until they entered the town.

"So what set you off? What has you acting, um, differently?"

"I went to a group therapy session for victims of abuse today. Well, no, I guess that was yesterday. Anyway, I heard some things I've never heard before. Really, the things I heard, I couldn't believe my ears. You see these stories on the news or whatever, and you don't think anything of it. But here I was with people who live right around here. They could be neighbors or relatives or people we work with, and they ... well, this one woman, she was telling these awful stories."

Robbie took his eyes off of the road for a moment to look at Ken, whose face showed little emotion.

"And last night, I swear, Robbie, if I don't show up at that house, a nineteen-year-old girl would be dead. You should have seen this guy. He was holding the cat up and saying he was going to kill the cat."

"Kill the cat?"

"Yeah. And poor Rhaymi, on the floor, crying her eyes out. There wasn't anything she could do. He would have smacked her all over the place if she tried to leave. In the least she was headed back to the hospital, if not the morgue."

"Jesus," Robbie sighed.

"Yeah, I know. But you know what really got me? What grabbed me by the heart and splattered it all over the ground was that last night, when I was at the state fair with my daughter and granddaughter, I learned my daughter was abused by one of her boyfriends."

"Brooke?"

"Yup."

"Really? Brooke?"

Raising his eyebrows, Robbie shot a long look at Ken, who peered back at him in return.

"Yeah, I know. Back in high school. I had no idea; I loved the kid. I used to drop hints they should get married. I mean, I thought I knew everything about my daughter. She was my only kid. I thought I paid attention. And then, bang, she tells me she dated this guy who was an absolute control freak. She said he'd get jealous and wanted to know where she was all the time, and who was she with. One night he grabbed her."

Ken dropped his head, taking his eyes off the road for the first time, rubbing his forehead with the palms of his hands.

"So my daughter's getting completely jerked around by this guy and I'm nudging her to marry him. I feel like such an awful dad. You know what I mean, Robbie?"

With his eyes back on the road, Ken waited for a reply, scratching his chin for a moment.

"Rob?"

Ken turned to his left. Robbie drove silently with two hands on the steering wheel and tears streaming down his face.

"Robbie, what's the matter? I'm sorry if I said something I … "

"It's OK, Ken. I've … I've had something pent up in me for a while."

"What is it, Rob?" Ken said, twisting his body toward his friend.

"So, you know Jennifer married another woman?"

"Yeah, of course. You told me all about the wedding. How long ago was that? Four, five years?"

"Almost five. So, well, when they first got married, Jennifer would say to me that her partner, Sierra, was suffocating her; always texting and wanting to know where she was."

Ken nodded, recalling Sierra's name.

"I told her that being married was an adjustment, that there was a lot of give-and-take in a marriage, and to give it time. That went on for about two years. Well, one day Jennifer told me Sierra picked up her cell phone and started looking at her text messages. I don't know why, but I snapped at Jennifer. I told her marriage isn't perfect and to suck it up and deal with it.

"Since then, she hasn't told me a thing. Whenever I ask how things are going, she says the same thing, 'Everything's fine.' But I know it isn't. I know. I can see it in Jennifer's face. She never smiles; her face is pale and thin; she never has any energy. And she was right - if Jennifer is at our house, Sierra constantly texts her. I mean, constantly. Jennifer went into the bathroom once, and I looked at her phone. She had six texts from Sierra in two minutes."

Robbie gripped the wheel before pounding the palm of his right hand on the dashboard.

"It's so frustrating!"

"So talk to her."

"I can't."

"Why not?"

"I can't, Ken. She doesn't want to talk to me."

"Sure she does."

"No, she doesn't. She has nothing to say when we see each other. We just talk about crap that doesn't matter – work, the weather, people we've bumped into here and there."

"That's not so bad."

"It is when you know your daughter is going through hell and you can't talk to her about it. My daughter's life sucks. I can see it in her eyes; I can see it on her face. And she won't talk to me about it because … ," Robbie's voice stopped, his right hand wiping away tears from his eyes.

"Why? Because why?"

Robbie's face tightened and his lips clamped closed before bursting open.

"Because I stuck up for the wrong person! I stuck up for the person who was jerking my daughter around. I should have stood up for my daughter, Ken. I should have protected my daughter. In the least, I should have just kept my mouth closed. But I didn't; I stood up for the person hurting my daughter, and now I've lost my daughter's trust. She won't talk to me. She doesn't tell me anything, and I know she's hurting inside, Ken. I know it."

"So talk to her."

"I can't."

"What do you mean you can't? You're her dad. You can talk to her anytime you want."

"She doesn't want to talk to me about that stuff. Haven't you heard a word I've said?"

"Yeah, I heard you. And I know if you *don't* say something she's going to end up like Rhaymi was last night – on the floor wondering if she is going to get killed."

Robbie's sobbing slowed down, and he glanced at Ken.

"You can't put your head in the sand, not on this one, Robbie. All right, maybe you screwed up a few years ago. So what? That's your daughter. Help your daughter; support your daughter. Don't ignore the problem, Robbie, because this problem's not going away."

Robbie nodded, taking another quick look at Ken before letting out a big sigh.

"What if she doesn't want to talk?"

"Yeah, yeah, that's a tough one. I tell ya, that group therapy was an eye opener yesterday. Oh my God, those poor people. But they're there, and they're talking. You could go to one of those therapy sessions, with Dr. Jonassen. You were right – she's great. They meet Friday afternoons. It's free."

Nodding again, Robbie's breathing returned mostly to normal

"OK. I don't know if Jennifer will talk to me or not, but she might go for a group therapy session."

"And you don't even have to talk if you don't want to. There was a young lady there yesterday; she didn't say a word. She just listened."

"Just listened? OK, if I tell her she doesn't even have to talk, I think she'll go."

Robbie turned his SUV left, and then took a quick right, slowing down on the neighborhood street.

"So, Ken, what are you going to do now?"

"What do you mean, now? Now as in when I get home in three minutes?"

"No, I mean, well, you've been through a lot here lately. Might be good to take a vacation; you know, get out of Dodge."

"Yeah, Robbie, that would probably be the smart thing to do, and maybe the healthy thing to do, too."

The lack of emotion returned to Ken's face.

"But I'm going to do the same thing you're going to do, Rob."

"What's that?"

"I'm going get my priorities in order, make a difference in this world, and help a person who needs help; a person who also happens to be someone I care about. Because, Robbie, I know if I don't, that person could end up dead."

Chapter 41

Ken tapped the front and back pockets of his pants feeling for his keys, and soon remembered he didn't have them. He pushed the buttons for the code to the garage, and the white door with three windows started climbing slowly. After stopping to take a deep breath in the kitchen, Ken marched up the stairs.

Fifteen minutes later, freshly showered and wearing a pair of gray sweatpants and a navy blue hoodie, Ken plopped himself into his reliable recliner. It was 6:01 p.m. The moment he pulled the chair's lever to put his feet up, the phone rang.

Dinga-linga-ling.

"Oh, come on," he mumbled.

Dinga-linga-ling.

Flipping the lever with his right hand, he popped out of his recliner and answered the phone in the kitchen.

"Hel ... ?"

"Ken, it's Robbie. Are you watching the news?" said his neighbor in a panicked voice.

"No, I just sat down. Why?"

"Put it on channel four. There's someone dead at the captain's son's house in Heapstown. They said it's a young woman."

Dropping the phone, Ken sprinted for the family room. He grabbed the clicker and turned on the TV, frantically pushing the channel button.

"So to recap," the middle-aged male newscaster said, "a person – a female – was found dead at eleven Birdie Lane in Heapstown late this afternoon. The homeowner is listed as Mathew O'Donnell, son of Pynchonton Police Captain Francis O'Donnell. Heapstown Police say foul play is not expected, and the name of the victim won't be released until the next of kin is notified. This is a developing story, and we hope to have more news for you at the eleven o'clock newscast."

Ken dropped the clicker and sprinted for the front door. Robbie walked quickly toward the house, his vehicle running at the end of the driveway.

"Come on, Ken. Get in," he said, turning around to get back into his SUV.

Racing out of the driveway, Robbie stomped on the gas pedal, causing the tires to squeal.

"He killed her, Robbie. The little bastard killed her."

"We don't know that. We don't know anything. We don't even know who's dead. I have a reporter on the way there right now and I told her to call me as soon as she finds out something."

Ken placed both hands on top of his head and firmly scratched, his face tense. Robbie's cell phone rang. He looked at the screen before pushing the green button on the phone, which sat in a plastic holder on the dashboard.

"Sarah, did you find out anything?" he asked from his seat. "Did the police talk to you?"

"Hi, Rob," replied the reporter on speakerphone. "Yes, no name yet, but it's a young female. They took her to Pynchonton Hospital."

"OK. Anything else?" Robbie asked.

"Not yet, other than no foul play and no one was home. The police said a neighbor found her at the front door unconscious."

"Great, Sarah. Keep me posted."

"You got it."

Rob pushed the red button and turned to his friend.

"No foul play, Ken."

"No, that's not true. He killed her. I know he did. He's around someplace, and I'm going to put a bullet between his eyes, like I should have last night."

"Ken, Jesus, don't talk like that."

"Rob, I was there last night. He wanted to kill her. He couldn't finish the job then because I was there, so he did it today."

Robbie took a hard right turn, forcing Ken to grab the handle of the door.

"Where are you going? This isn't the way to Heapstown."

"Hospital," Rob quickly answered. "My reporter will call me if any more news comes from the house. The body is at the hospital That's where we'll get our answer."

Chapter 42

The familiar glass double doors automatically opened as Ken and Robbie approached the hospital's emergency room entrance.

"A girl was brought here a little while ago. I need to see her," Ken insisted.

"Are you related, Sir?" a forty-something-year-old male at the front desk asked.

"Related? No. She doesn't have any relatives in the area."

"OK. What's the name and I will have the nurse ask the patient if they would like to see you. What's your name?"

"My name? My name is Ken Roy. But the patient ... the patient I want to see is dead," answered Ken, his voice close to frantic.

"Excuse me?"

"Someone was brought here, to the hospital. I think I know who it is, but I'm not sure. I just want to see the body."

"Oh, Sir, I'm sorry. We can't allow that."

"But who's going to identify the body? Her boyfriend? Her boyfriend is the one who killed her."

The volunteer, looked to his left, then his right, searching for some way to appease Ken.

"Sir, I'm sorry, but I can't let you … ahh … I can't let you do anything. We'll take care of it here."

"Take care of it? How? No one here knows who she is," Ken said, hitting the palm of his hand on top of the chest-high desk.

"We have people here who can take care of it."

Ken snapped his shoulders away from the desk before smacking his hands together.

"What can we do, Robbie?"

"Tricky one; I'm not sure," he said, pausing before he continued. "Here, let me call the copy desk and get another reporter down here?"

"Isn't there one already here?"

"No, just Sarah at the house."

"Robbie, I think there's one already here."

"Where? Who?" asked Robbie, looking throughout the room.

"Got your press pass on you?"

"Oh, geez. Ha. Yup, right here in my wallet. Never leave home without it."

"OK. Rob, you've got to get us back there. Think you can do it?"

"Yeah, but not with us; just me."

Ken frowned, not understanding why his friend would not include him.

"You don't have a camera, and you're a little old to be an intern, Ken. I can't get you in there. I'll take this one by myself."

With a pat on Ken's shoulder, Robbie walked through the waiting room and into the long hallway. Ken paced and paced in the waiting area, his head reacting to every movement and sound. He froze, his head up. Quickly, he walked toward the big, metal double door that led to inside the hospital.

"Maria!"

"Hey, Ken! Hey, it's great to see you. You volunteering nights now?"

"Hi, Maria," said Ken, lowering his voice so the man at the front desk couldn't hear. "No, something else has popped up."

"Is someone you know here?"

Ken hesitated, grabbing his chin and looking at the man at the front desk before replying.

"Yes. Yes, someone I know is here."

"Would you like to see them?"

"Yeah, I really would, Maria. It's a touchy situation."

"OK, Ken. Wait here."

Maria walked to the back of the front desk, opened a drawer, and grabbed a white sticker that read "Guest" on it. She carefully placed it on the chest of Ken's hoodie.

"There, Ken. You all set now."

"Thanks, Maria."

"You welcome, Ken. You such a nice man."

"Hey, Maria?"

"Yes, Ken."

"I could use your help."

Chapter 43

The metal double doors closed behind Ken and Maria. Still in just his socks, Ken walked silently along the tile, and Maria did the same in her red crocs.

"Where are we going, Ken?"

"I don't know."

"Then why are we walking?"

"I don't know. I just am."

"Well, who are you looking for?"

Ken stopped suddenly, tapping the fingers of his right hand on his lips.

"Maria, I have a bit of an odd question for you, but it's an important question."

"What is it?"

"Where … where does the hospital keep dead bodies?"

"Dead bodies?"

"Yeah."

"Why?"

"You know how you asked me if I was here to see someone I know?"

"Yes."

"Well, I think that person might be dead."

"Was it a relative?"

"No."

"Don't tell me it was that pretty, young girl I seen you with a while ago. Please don't tell me it was her."

"I think it is."

Maria covered her mouth with both hands, stomping her right foot on the ground once, and then two more times back-to-back. Maria grabbed Ken by the wrist.

"Come on. I know where they at."

With purpose, Maria led Ken down one hall, and then another, and then another. Right turn, left turn, right turn, left turn into a part of the hospital Ken had never been. The two approached a set of gray double doors. Maria pressed a button with her left hand, propelling the doors open. A police officer stood in the hallway. Ken and Maria slowly walked into the area. Another officer stepped out of a room as the door behind them closed. Maria, still attached to Ken's wrist, walked into the room where the officer had just exited. A female nurse moved medical equipment away from a gurney, which had a white sheet on it.

"The body is under there, Ken," Maria said, pointing.

Ken stood still, staring at the white sheet.

"Do you want me to look? I think I'd know what she looks like."

Shaking his head slightly, Ken gently tugged his hand away from Maria's wrist and cautiously stepped toward the figure. He took a deep breath, let out a long sigh, carefully grabbed the end of the sheet with his left hand and pulled it back.

It was Rhaymi.

Ken closed his eyes and clenched his teeth, his lips pressing together tighter and tighter. He stayed perfectly still before placing the sheet back over Rhaymi's lifeless face, opening his eyes and turning as he looked at Maria.

"I'm sorry, Ken."

With tears in his eyes, Ken nodded as he stepped into the hallway, his thoughts scattered. He stared at the white-tiled floor until a voice caught his ear. He recognized it, but not well. He took three cautious steps and looked to his right down a hall. His head shot up and he stomped down the hall.

"Hey!"

Captain O'Donnell turned, squaring his broad shoulders and advancing toward Ken.

"What are you doing here? You aren't authorized to be in here."

"Authorized?" questioned Ken, now chest-to-chest with the captain and displaying the same confidence he showed at the police station. "Your son tortures and kills an innocent girl, and you're telling me about being authorized?"

"My son didn't kill anyone."

"That's a lie!" Ken yelled, sticking his finger into the captain's chest. "He almost killed her last night and he finished the job today. I should have popped your kid between the eyes when I had the chance."

"You want to talk about poppin' someone?" barked the captain in return. "I'll tell you about poppin' someone, Buddy."

"Apple doesn't fall far from the tree, Captain!" Ken yelled.

"Ken, Captain O'Donnell, knock it off," said Robbie, stepping between the two fuming men. "Keep it down. You're in a hospital for Christ's sake."

The men retreated, a small crowd of officers and hospital staff surrounding them.

"You know he killed her," Ken continued, his voice lowered.

"He didn't kill her," the captain replied.

"Don't cover up for him. Do your job. Your son killed Rhaymi."

"My son's in Las Vegas."

The comment stunned Ken, who frowned, looked at the floor and then back at the captain.

"Las Vegas? You're lying."

"No, he's not, Ken."

Ken quickly spun toward Robbie, who was holding a white piece of paper and pen in his hand.

"Captain O'Donnell's son boarded a flight from New England Airport at eight this morning. He had a direct flight and landed at McCarran International Airport in Las Vegas around noon Eastern Standard Time. We have confirmed with the Las Vegas police and casino security that Mathew is in Las Vegas as we speak."

'That can't be true. He must have killed her last night and left this morning."

"Sorry, Ken. The doctor just told me she died about four hours ago, so around three in the afternoon; the neighbor found her on the front step. No foul play."

"No foul play? What do you mean no foul play? People don't just die. Nineteen year olds don't just die on front steps. Someone had to kill her."

"No one killed her, Ken."

Ken spun around at the unexpected female voice. It was Dr. Harding, dressed in her standard white lab coat. The psychologist gently looked into Ken's eyes.

"It was an overdose."

Chapter 44

Ken turned and lowered himself into the same chair he sat in seven weeks earlier, as Dr. Harding softly closed the door and sat behind her desk.

"What happened?" Ken asked, his shoulders slumped and his hands clasped between his thighs.

"A neighbor saw a young woman at the house, crying on the front step late this morning. A few hours later that same neighbor saw her again and thought she was sleeping on the front step, so he went over to check. He found Rhaymi dead, there on the front step."

Blinking, Ken dropped his head.

"He called the police right away. He never saw anyone else at the house – just your car in the driveway."

"My car?" Ken said, surprised.

"Silver Camry? Massachusetts plates?"

"Ahh, yeah."

"No worries, Ken. The Heapstown Police know Rhaymi took your car after the Pynchonton Police pulled you over last night. They never suspected you."

Nodding, Ken pinched the bridge of his nose.

"So what do you think happened?"

"Well, we know Rhaymi was in her dorm late last night. We confirmed that with her roommate and R.A. The boyfriend left this morning; we know that as well. I'm guessing he texted her something this morning that made her feel worse than she already felt, she went over there, probably after he left, and ... I don't know. The police found a bottle of Tylenol PM - a container of 325 capsules - empty on the ground."

"Tylenol?" Ken questioned."

"Yes. There's nothing wrong with taking Tylenol, but it can easily be misused because it can be purchased over the counter. She probably took the entire bottle."

"So you don't think Captain O'Donnell covered anything up?"

"Nope. He was never at the house, and the doctor and I saw Ehaymi here long before he arrived at the hospital. It was an overdose, Ken, plain and simple."

"And the boyfriend, Mathew. Looks like he was in Las Vegas, so I guess he's clean."

"Well, he was in Vegas, but he's not clean."

"What do you mean?"

The doctor stood and moved in front of her desk, leaning against it.

"He didn't physically kill Rhaymi; he didn't place his hands around her neck or shoot her or anything, but in a sense, he did kill her. No question – he killed her. Broke her down into nothing; I've seen it so many times."

"You know I was at the house the night before, and walked in while Mathew was hollering at Rhay," Ken explained.

"No, Ken. I didn't know that."

"Yeah. He was holding the cat carrier up with the cat in it, threatening to hurt it. Rhaymi was on the floor crying. And then he said he was going to throw … "

" … throw her out the window?"

"Yeah. How'd you know?"

"I've been doing this a long time, Ken. Got my practicing license thirty-two years ago. I've seen a lot in my years. Not everything, but a lot, and I've seen this one all too often. Poor girl."

"I thought she was making progress. She stayed with me for a week, studying for her finals, and … and she seemed great."

"Oh, that was nice of you to let her stay with you at your home. You probably took a load off her mind and just let her focus on being a college kid."

"Yeah, that's what it seemed like."

"Yes, well, abuse victims are very good at putting up fronts and hiding what they don't want people to see. They can go about their day and you might not even have a hint of a clue that there is something wrong, when in fact they're all just soaked paper towels."

"Soaked paper towels?"

"Yes. You know how most relationships start out great; you know, the honeymoon phase?"

"I've never heard of that phrase, but I think I know what you're getting at."

"OK, well picture one of the people as a paper towel. The paper towel is strong and sturdy in the honeymoon phase. And then one little thing goes wrong, so add one tiny drop of water to the paper towel. No problem; the paper towel can absorb that one drop of water. And let's be realistic, there are ups and downs in most relationships, so, yes, the paper towel takes on some water here and there, but it can handle it."

Ken nodded, interested in Dr. Harding's metaphor.

"But in an abusive relationship … "

" … there's a lot of water," Ken continued.

"Exactly. There's a lot of water. The problems start out just as drips, just like any other relationship. But the drips start to come more often, and the paper towel works to absorb all the water. And then the drips are coming all the time – day after day, month after month, year after year. After a while, the paper towel just can't absorb the water anymore. The water takes over, and there's nothing the paper towel can do."

"Rhaymi drowned."

"Yes, in a sense."

Ken looked down, tapping his fingertips together before looking back up.

"Anything we can do?"

"I'm afraid not. The boyfriend wasn't home at the time of death; not even in the same state. I'm pretty sure I know what he did to Rhaymi while they were dating, but we have no witnesses to actual physical abuse, and Rhaymi never pressed any charges against him. Sorry, Ken, but we're stuck."

Ken nodded as he stood up and shook hands with the doctor, who gave him a small smile in return.

Silently, Ken walked toward the door and opened it.

"Ken," said Dr. Harding as he stood in the doorway. "Rhaymi was lucky to have you as a friend."

Chapter 45

A light *click* repeating over and over was the only sound in the house, as Ken slowly rocked back-and-forth in his recliner. The family room grew darker, with the sun setting well after dinner. He stared with half-open eyes, his head tilted to the left. Back-and-forth, back-and-forth he swayed.

Knock-knock; knock-knock.

Pushing his hands against the arms of the chair, Ken stood and slowly walked to the door, his socks barely lifting off the floor. Without looking through the window, he opened the door.

"Hey, Ken."

"Hi, Robbie."

"Haven't seen you in a few days. You doing OK?"

"Yeah, I'm fine."

"Mind if I come in?"

Ken stepped back. Robbie gave him a slight smile and walked into the kitchen."

"You have time to talk?" Robbie asked. Ken nodded in return. "I'm a little worried about you."

"Yeah, why's that?"

"Well, you're usually on the move. Running in the morning, driving around to do some errands, yard work. Your yard puts everyone else's in the neighborhood to shame, and we all have professional landscapers."

Ken walked into the family room and settled into his recliner, his head tilted upward as he resumed his rocking.

"You're an on-the-go kind of guy, Ken. But no one has seen you the last four days. I don't think your car has moved. Have you left the house at all?"

"No."

"My wife said she hasn't seen you at all – not in the yard; not ever getting the mail."

Robbie sat down in the nearest chair and popped up immediately, remembering that was where Marie sat. He shuffled his feet and positioned himself in the center of the couch.

"I understand if you're upset about this girl dying. I do. It sounds like you two had a nice relationship – a mentoring relationship. But you didn't act like this when your friend Dan died, and you didn't act like this when Marie died. You were your old self; right back out there doing all the things you do."

Ken nodded, agreeing with Robbie's statement.

"So I was wondering why are you in such a funk now? What's different about this?"

The recliner continued to gently move back-and-forth. Ken took his eyes off the wall and looked at Robbie, who patiently waited for a reply.

"Spouses die. Mine died much earlier than I expected, but I always knew there was a 50-50 chance I would have to live without Marie. And when she was diagnosed with ALS, well, I knew our time together was coming to an end. Same with Danny. I knew him for almost my entire life. We were best friends for, geez, I don't know, sixty years. Still, I knew I might have to go to his funeral someday, and when he was diagnosed with his brain tumor, I knew I'd be burying my best friend.

"But with Rhaymi, see, here's the thing," Ken continued, shifting in his seat to give Robbie his full attention. "Nineteen-year-olds don't die, Robbie, OK? They don't die. To lose Rhaymi, even with all the problems she had, I didn't see that one coming. She shouldn't be dead."

Robbie nodded, dropping his head as he looked at the coffee table in front of him.

"But that wasn't the hardest part," Ken continued, drawing Robbie's gaze again. "You want to know the hardest part; the part that has had a strangle hold on me for four days?

Ken stood, squeezing his face from top to bottom with his hands.

"I didn't get to say goodbye."

Robbie pursed his lips and nodded, understanding Ken's feelings.

"I got to say goodbye to Marie and Danny. Their deaths hurt; they really hurt. But I got to say goodbye."

Sticking his hands in his pockets, Ken looked at his ceiling.

"I didn't get to say goodbye to Rhaymi."

The room was perfectly quiet, and it stayed that way for a minute until Robbie stood.

"You want to say goodbye?" Robbie asked.

Ken turned toward his friend, hesitating before replying, "Yeah, I would."

"OK, let's see what we can do." Robbie stepped around the coffee table and pulled out the folding chair at the small desk in the corner of the room before sitting down.

"God, how old is this computer?" Robbie asked, pushing the button on the tower for the desktop.

"Oh, I don't know. Marie bought that a while ago."

"Do you use it?"

"Not really."

The screen brightened, and Robbie responded by typing on the keyboard.

"Do you use Safari or Chrome?"

"What?"

"Safari or Chrome, you know, for your browser."

Ken looked blankly at his friend at the desk.

"Never mind. It doesn't matter."

Robbie maneuvered his fingers along the keyboard for a few seconds.

"What was Rhaymi's last name?"

"Summers."

"Do you know where she was from?"

"California. Malibu."

Robbie continued to type before putting the tip of his right index finger on the screen.

"Here it is. Rhaymi Destiny Summers, Malibu, California, died May 17 ... ahh, daughter of Savannah Summers ... let's see ... ahh, funeral services for family and close friends only on May 23 from 1-3 p.m. at Martin Funeral Home in Malibu. Private burial."

Robbie tapped the screen twice before turning to his friend.

"You wanna go?"

"Go?"

"Yeah, go; go to California to the funeral. It said close friends. I'm sure if you explained yourself to Rhaymi's mom she wouldn't mind if you attended."

"California?"

"Yeah, California."

"We can't get to California in two days. I don't think a travel agent could find anything that quickly."

"Travel agent? No one uses a travel agent anymore."

"Well, we can't drive to California in two days."

"Ken, good God, get with the times, Buddy."

Robbie spent another minute clicking away on the computer.

"Bingo. Here, we can be in SoCal by noon their time tomorrow."

"Tomorrow? How?"

"How do you think we could get there tomorrow?"

"A plane? But you didn't call anyone! You didn't call an airline, or use your eyes phone like Brooke did."

"Ken," Robbie said, shaking his head. "You can just go to a website and see which flights are available."

"Really?"

"No, I'm making that up. Yes, Ken. Yes. Here, U.S.A. Airlines, leaves New England Airport at nine in the morning tomorrow; direct flight to L.A. It's a little more than $350 round trip."

"Oh, that doesn't sound so bad."

"No, that's fair. You'll just need to get a rental car to drive to Malibu. It isn't far. Do you want me to book it?"

Ken stepped back, putting his hands in his pockets and rocking back-and-forth on his feet.

"Yeah, Robbie. That's a good idea. Thanks."

"For one or two?"

"What do you mean?"

"One ticket or two? Do you want me to go along with you?"

Ken tugged on his chin one, two, three, four times.

"I think I should go alone on this one, Rob. Thanks."

Chapter 46

Zzzzzzzip.

Ken closed the red backpack at his feet after pulling out the book Robbie lent him. Before the plane taxied to the runway, Ken was eleven pages into *The Abusive Relationship*, a New York Times Bestseller by Dr. Kimberly Cooper. The hardcover included all of the topics covered at the group therapy session, including the gaslighting.

The fourth chapter, titled War with Words, though, confused Ken at first. The chapter explained how verbal abuse, often meaning manipulation, slowly chipped away at the victim's self-esteem. What caught Ken off guard, however, was how verbal abuse can be as dangerous as physical abuse, and the two don't always go hand-in-hand. Ken believed one always had to do with another, with verbal abuse often the precursor to a physical altercation. Not true, Ken learned.

Throughout the flight, Ken routinely spoke to himself; granted, often in one- or two-word comments so no one could hear. Name-calling, criticizing, blaming, threats – all typically done one-on-one so an outsider couldn't see or cast a judgment. Manipulating; twisting; it was all about control - one person controlling the other. The idea Ken found most fascinating was that verbal abuse was just as dangerous as physical abuse, and even harder to detect than physical abuse.

"Of course," he muttered.

Ken shook his head at a number of the common phrases in the chapter on verbal abuse, having never been in an unhealthy relationship as a husband, father or friend.

- "You don't really feel like that."

- "You should stop being so sensitive."

- "You're making me act like this."

- "If you really loved me you wouldn't have done that."

- "Are you trying to start an argument?"

- "You're ruining our relationship."

- "Why do you have to blow everything out of proportion?"

Ken plowed through the 198-page self-help book, closing it just as the plane put its landing gear down. He stared straight ahead. at the back of the seat roughly a foot in front of him.

The flight landed on time. Ken grabbed his suitcase, rented his car, and drove west to Malibu, pulling into the parking lot of the Pegasus Hotel & Suites by early afternoon. Since the plane touched down, he had been in a fog, processing all of this new, disturbing information. For someone who had led a simple, conflict-free life for six-plus decades, the material was a lot to handle.

Ken's haze lifted when he stepped out of his rental car, a yellow Dodge Charger. It was not at all his style, but it was all that was available on short notice. The warm breeze snapped him out of his funk. He could smell the Pacific Ocean. He closed his eyes and sucked in the salt air.

With his backpack slung over his right shoulder, he carried his suitcase into the hotel. There was a small, marble fountain in the middle of the foyer; water streamed out of the mouth of a Pegasus, its front feet high in the air. Ken smiled at the figure, leaning forward and touching the smooth stone.

Snap. Bang.

Ken's backpack fell off his shoulder and onto the white floor. The stitching at the top of the strap had given way. He inspected the strap, glancing up as a couple a generation younger than him walked into the foyer. The woman stopped abruptly, clutching a man Ken assumed was her husband or boyfriend on the forearm.

"Why can't you just buy a pair of sunglasses?" the woman snapped in a forceful whisper. A pair of round sunglasses rested on top of her long, brown hair.

The man put his hands in his pockets and shrugged his shoulders.

"Why are you being so stubborn about this?"

"Honey, I'm not being stubborn," the husband calmly replied "I forgot mine back home and I don't want to spend a bunch of money on something I don't need."

"You *are* being stubborn. You always act like this."

Triggers started to go off in Ken. He didn't look up, but the conversation had caught his attention.

"Why do you act like that? All the time, you act like that."

"Honey, I just forgot my sunglasses. It's no big deal."

"Don't tell me what is and isn't a big deal. I know what is and isn't a big deal. And what's a big deal is your ruining my vacation."

The husband let out a long sigh, his head dropping.

"See, there you go. It's the same thing all the time, Joseph. Why do you do that? Do you want me to have fun on vacation? Do you?"

The husband nodded, his eyes fixed on the marble floor.

"Can you just buy the sunglasses, please?"

The husband's nod never stopped.

"Thank you, Joseph," said the wife, putting her right palm on her husband's left cheek. "Now, I'm going to check us in and then we're going to go get you some sunglasses while we're shopping. And then we'll go walk along the beach before a nice dinner."

The wife turned and walked around the fountain to the front desk. For the first time, Ken glanced up at the man, who stood motionless with his hands still in his pockets. Ken looked at his backpack before quickly placing his right hand on his mouth. He stayed that way for a few seconds before unzipping his backpack and taking out the book. It's red cover and black letters stood out boldly.

Standing, Ken held the book in his left hand. He took three strides and stretched out his arm, holding the book a foot away from the man's belt buckle. The man looked at the cover; the title was easy to see. He breathed one, two, three times before slowing taking his right hand out of his pocket and reaching for the book. He stopped, his eyes turning toward Ken for the first time.

"I just finished it," Ken calmly said.

The man closed his eyes for an extended blink before carefully clutching the hardcover.

"It's a good book," Ken continued.

The man let out a long sigh, scratching the outside corner of his left eye as Ken stepped away and walked to the front desk to check in.

Chapter 47

Ken thought his Dodge Charger was a little on the showy side until he pulled into the parking lot at Martin Funeral Home. He parked in a far corner, afraid of driving anywhere near any of the luxury vehicles. He adjusted his collar and buttoned his brown suit before walking toward the entrance. The first car he spotted was a black Mercedes, then a white Range Rover, another black Mercedes, a red Ferrari, and a navy blue Bentley. His stride slowed when he walked by a Lamborghini.

"Wow."

Through the parked cars, Ken approached two well-built young men in black suits standing at the base of the steps, their hands folded at the waist.

"Sir, are you a family member?" the young man on the left said.

"No, I'm not," replied Ken, thinking the man's tone was a tad harsh.

"Then are you close friend of Mrs. Summers?"

"I was very close with Rhaymi, where she went to college."

The two men looked at each other before both sizing up Ken.

"Sir, this is a private funeral."

"Yes, I know. I flew here from Massachusetts to pay my respects to Mrs. Summers. Rhaymi was a remarkable young woman."

Again, the men looked Ken up and down, while Ken stood with his hands in his pockets. "OK. Up the stairs and straight ahead," the man on the left said, his face stern.

"Thank you," Ken said as he trotted up the four steps.

A man, much slimmer and a generation older than the men outside, opened the glass door.

"Good day, Sir. If you need any assistance, please do not hesitate to approach me or my brothers," the man said, gesturing toward two other professionally-dressed men in their forties near the entrance of a room. "We want you to feel as comfortable as possible while you are here today at Martin Funeral Home."

"Why, thank you. That's nice of you to say," Ken answered, admiring the multiple paintings on the wall, as well as a low-hanging chandelier.

"Would you like a drink of water, Sir?"

"Ahh, yeah, sure."

The light-footed man stepped to his right and quickly pulled the tap of a glass container, and the water flowed into a small plastic cup.

"Here, Sir."

"Thank you."

Ken carefully pinched the cup, which was only slightly bigger than a shot glass. He tilted his head and poured all of the drink into his mouth. He held the cup to his lips, looking at it as he kept his head back. He looked at the man, who stood smiling from ear-to-ear. Ken slowly gulped, trying not to make a face of disgust. He handed the cup to the man, who carefully grabbed it and placed it into what Ken thought was a vase on the floor.

"That was water?"

"Yes, Sir. The best in Southern California."

"OK, if you say so."

"We'll be sure to have some available tomorrow at the burial. It's supposed to be hotter than usual for this time of year."

"Where's the burial? I didn't see anything on that yet."

"Oh, well, maybe because it's not in Malibu. It's in Westwood. Marilyn Monroe is buried in the same cemetery."

"You're kidding?"

"No, along with many other famous people. Who knows, Rhaym could be between Dean Martin and Natalie Wood. The burial should be quite the spectacle."

Ken nodded, his eyebrows high.

"Of course, you know this will be a private burial. It's for family members and guests of Mrs. Summers only."

"I'll be sure to talk to her about it inside."

"Right, Sir."

"Thank you," said Ken, shaking the man's hand. "I guess I'll go pay my respects."

Grinning as he walked toward the room, he stopped as he reached the archway. His smile slowly evaporated. Dozens of vases and stands with lily flowers framed the room. There was no line; no casket. Most of the people were in their thirties or forties, Ken guessed. The men wore cashmere or silk-looking suits, while the women were dressed in tight-fitting attire. The twenty or so people in the room seemed a few notches too jovial, in Ken's opinion. He thought the scene resembled a Christmas party more than a funeral.

Taking one step forward, Ken scanned the room. He looked all along the outskirts of the floor and along the walls, through the cheerful guests. Scratching his head, Ken left the room and went back to the man at the door.

"Is that the calling hours for Rhaymi Summers?"

"Why, yes, Sir. It is."

"Are you sure?" Ken asked.

"Yes, Sir. We have just the one room."

"Then why aren't there any pictures of Rhaymi?"

"I don't know, Sir. You'll have to ask Mrs. Summers. She's inside, wearing the white dress with the matching hat."

Confused, Ken walked back to the archway. A slim woman dressed in a white, thigh-high outfit and a black-rimmed white hat talked to a couple who appeared to be a few years older and very athletic-looking, like everyone else in the room. Ken inspected the rest of the people, and didn't see anyone who fit the woman's description. Another couple joined the conversation. The group laughed. Ken thought he heard someone say something about crazy rich Asians, but figured he must have misheard.

After fifteen minutes or so, four people hugged someone Ken believed was Mrs. Summers and walked through the archway. He stepped forward, putting his right hand up to get the woman's attention. Noticing, she stood still as Ken approached.

"Mrs. Summers?"

"Yes," she replied cautiously.

"Hi, I'm Ken Roy. I'm a friend of Rhaymi's."

"Ken Roy? I don't know a Ken Roy."

"No, we haven't met before. I'm from Massachusetts, where Rhaymi went to college."

"Are you a Dean at the college, or a professor?"

"Oh, neither. I don't work at the college."

"Then how did Rhaymi know you?"

"I'm just a friend."

"Mr. Roy, this ceremony is for family and close friends."

"Oh, Rhaymi and I were close; very close. I met her when I was volunteering at the hospital. We ran a marathon together, and I let her stay at my house when she was studying for her finals."

Mrs. Summers placed both of her hands on her hips and cocked her head back.

"What are you talking about, Mr. Roy. Hospital? Marathon? And what do you mean she stayed at your house?"

"Mrs. Summers, it's nothing strange. She, ahh, she was getting abused by her boyfriend. She just ... she just needed a safe place to stay so she could study and not have any distractions."

"That girl was nothing but a distraction. Her whole life, it was one thing after another."

Ken paused, struggling to process the comment.

"Mrs. Summers, did you know your daughter was being abused by her boyfriend?" Ken politely asked. "It's OK if you didn't know, but she *was* being abused. I know; I saw it with my own two eyes."

"Mr. Roy the only people who get abused are people who *want* to get abused. If she was in an unhealthy relationship, that's her own fault."

"No, Mrs. Summers, I'm sorry, but that's not true. Most people don't even know when they're in an abusive relationship, and when they do realize it they often feel trapped – like they can't get out. That man Rhaymi was dating completely manipulated her. He had her wrapped around his finger. He had all the control."

"All she had to do was leave. It's not that difficult."

"Ahh, yeah, it is. It's very difficult," Ken continued, challenging the comment. "I don't think you understand what type of situation Rhaymi was in."

"I understood my daughter perfectly well, thank you."

"Really? Do you know she was in the hospital four times in the last few months? Do you know her life was so out of control she drove her car into a tree? Do you know the night before she died her boyfriend threatened to throw her out of a second story window? Did you know any of that?"

Mrs. Summers crossed her arms, looking away before scowling back at Ken.

"I don't answer to you, Mr. Roy. I answer to me, and that's it. I don't know how someone like you got in here in the first place, but your stay here is over. Off you go, Mr. Roy.

Looking at the guests who had surrounded Mrs. Summers during their conversation, Ken gave a single nod to the hostess, turned, and walked out of the room through the archway.

Mrs. Summers and her friends rolled their eyes and shook their heads, disgusted by Ken's presence. Mrs. Summers mimicked Ken, raising her right hand up and putting it on her forehand, with her thumb and index finger in the shape of an "L."

"You don't have to answer to me, Mrs. Summers; you don't have the answer to me," Ken repeated, storming back into the room with his right arm fully extended and his finger pointed directly at Mrs. Summers. "But you do have to answer to Rhaymi.

"Your daughter needed you. Your daughter needed a mom, a parent. But you weren't there. You were never there. You said Rhaymi was a distraction? Yeah, it's hard being a parent. It takes a lot of effort. It's work; work you weren't willing to do."

"You're not welcome here."

"That's the same message you gave to Rhaymi. You quit on her; you quit on your own kid. Times got tough, and instead of trying to help your daughter, you ignored her. That's why she went to college more than 2,000 miles away from home. She didn't feel welcomed in her own house."

"That's enough, Mr. Roy. Trevor, you and your brothers escort this man outside, back to Massachusetts where he came from.'

"At least back in Massachusetts she had one person who cared about her, which is more than I can say about this place. Rhaymi's dead, and there isn't one photograph of her; no casket; no memorabilia; none of her friends. This is all about you. This thing is all about you. No wonder she wanted to go to college so far from home."

"Trevor!" she barked.

"You can kick me out; go ahead. But if you ever wonder why your daughter is dead, the answer is right in the mirror."

Ken felt a weak grip on his right bicep. He quickly spun, grabbing Trevor by his bowtie, then jammed his left hand into the man's throat.

"Let go," Ken fumed, his teeth clenched, "or I will take you for everything you have."

The owner loosened his grip and lowered his hand. Ken did the same, tugging at the end of his left sleeve. He walked toward the archway, turned halfway around at the crowd and said, "Someone had to speak for Rhaymi."

Chapter 48

Ken held his flip phone to his left ear as he paced in his seventh-floor hotel room.

"Hello?"

"Hi, Sweetie."

"Hi, Daddy," Brooke said. "I tried calling you at home all day yesterday and you didn't answer. Are you OK?"

"Yeah. I flew to California. I wanted to go to Rhaymi's funeral."

"California? Daddy, you've never traveled that far away from home before."

"Yeah, I know."

"Well, that was nice of you to go. I'm sure her family appreciates you flying all that way."

"Not exactly."

"What do you mean?"

"Never mind. I'll tell you another time."

"OK. So, Daddy, I'm worried about you. You've had so many things happen to you within the last year – first Mr. Huber dying, and then Mom, then you retired, and now this."

"Yeah, it's been a lot."

"So do you know what you're going to do?"

"No, I'm still sorting that out."

"OK, well, you need to do something. You're not good at doing nothing."

"Ha, you got that right. I might be the worst laziest person in the world."

Ken walked toward the window. He noticed the husband and wife he had seen the day before in the lobby outside. They were walking from their car to the hotel, and the wife was talking with her hands flailing.

"Hey, Sweetie. One thing I have been thinking about is you and Ricky Taylor dating in high school. I … I'm sorry I didn't help you. I … I don't feel like a very good father right now."

"Daddy, that was so long ago."

"Yeah, I know, but I wasn't there for you. You needed help, and I didn't do anything to help you."

"It's not your fault. You didn't know; I didn't tell you. If anyone is to blame, it's me for not telling you or Mom."

"No, I'm a parent. I should be able to pick up on things; things like when your daughter is in a bad relationship. I just didn't see it."

"No damage done, Daddy. It all worked out."

"Yeah, OK. Hey, how's Celina doing today? What's she up to?"

"She's crawling all over the place; she gets into everything. It's not so bad inside, but when we're outside, she gets sand all over her hands, and there are bugs and snakes outside."

"Snakes?"

"Yeah. We haven't seen any, but our neighbor came across a cottonmouth near the pond next to his yard last week. They can get pretty big, and they're poisonous."

"Poisonous?"

"Yeah."

Ken rubbed his hand back-and-forth across his hair, with his eyes wide open.

"How much longer will you be in California, Daddy?"

"Just one more night. My flight leaves Los Angeles at seven at night. I don't know what I'm going to do all day. I was planning on going to the burial in the morning."

"So why don't you?"

"I'm not invited."

"Not invited? But you flew all the way there."

"Yeah, it's just for family and close friends of Mrs. Summers."

"Oh, OK. Hey, Daddy. I'm going to hang up now. Celina is standing up and pulling on one of the gates we have at the top of the stairs. We haven't figured out how to secure that to the wall the right way and I'm afraid she's going to fall down the stairs."

"Ahh, yeah, yeah. Go; take care of that. I'll call you when I get home."

"OK. Bye, Daddy. Love you."

"Love you, too, Sweetie."

Ken hung up the phone, then squeezed his face with his right hand as he looked out the window at the blue sky. He kept his hand over his mouth, standing still for minutes.

Suddenly, Ken spun around and left the room. He returned five minutes later with a white envelope in his hand. He pulled the rolling chair back and sat at the black desk. He moved the hotel's pad of paper in front of him before opening the center drawer and taking out a black pen. He placed the envelope in front of him, turning it horizontally. He wrote in big, capital letters:

TO CELINA

OPEN WHEN YOU ARE 16

Ken pushed the envelope to the top of the desk, sliding the pad under his right hand. He began to write:

Dear Celina,

Hi. It's Grampy. Since you're reading this that means you are 16 years old. Your birthday might be today. If today is your birthday, happy birthday!

Since you're 16, that means you're old enough to date other people. Maybe you have already begun dating. Dating can be a lot of fun. You get to do exciting things and go to neat places with someone you care about. That's fun!!! But dating can also be confusing. Sometimes people might say or do things you don't understand. And sometimes, someone you are dating might try to hurt you. Hopefully that will never happen to you, but if someone ever harms you in any way, I want you to do one thing: tell your parents immediately. They can help you. And you'll have to trust me on this one - you will be glad you told them. I knew a girl whose boyfriend grabbed her and always made her feel bad. I knew another girl whose boyfriend slapped her time and time again. I don't want that to happen to you. You're an angel. If someone hurts you, can you promise me you will tell your parents for me, please? Can you make that promise to Grampy? If you say yes, you will make Grampy happy.

Celina, I don't know if I'll be alive when you read this. But if I'm gone, that's OK because that means I'm with Grammy in heaven. I miss Grammy.

Grammy and Grampy love you.

Love,

Grampy

Chapter 49

A quick stop at eight in the morning at the Westwood Chamber of Commerce was all Ken needed to find the correct cemetery. Slouched in the leather driver's seat of the Dodge Charger, his eyes looking just over the steering wheel, he watched from where he had parked along the road as Mrs. Summers and her guests walked away from the plot to their limousines and drove away.

Once Rhaymi's mom and her friends were out of sight, he stepped out of the rental car, which had begun to heat up in the late morning sun. He moved slowly, his body stiff from sitting still for more than three hours. Ken didn't want to be disrespectful by going to the burial when he wasn't invited, or to be on site when the family arrived. However, he wanted to pay his final respects to his friend, and with his flight departing in seven hours, this was his opportunity to say goodbye to Rhaymi.

With his hands in his coat pockets, Ken strolled along the sidewalk parallel with the chest-high, wrought iron fence. He could see the entrance coming into view. Two gray stone pillars stood ten feet high, and the cement walkway turned to red brick.

He walked past a dozen or so marble headstones, all dated from the early 1900s. He turned left, heading toward where he saw the small crowd gathered for Rhaymi's burial. The monuments along the bricks were grossly oversized, in his opinion; some stood much taller than Ken. He knew Rhaymi was near the end of the walkway, along the outside border of the property. The headstones were deep in this section, with no paths. He reached the end, where the branches of an oak tree on the other side of the fence reached over and gave shade to the nearby markers.

Spotting fresh dirt, he hesitantly stepped onto the grass between the fence and last headstone. He walked by five plots before reaching Rhaymi's, which was smaller than the others in the area. Knee-high and roughly two feet wide, the black granite stone read:

Rhaymi Destiny Summers

B: August 15, 1998

D: May 17, 2018

With his shoulders squared, and his arms folded, Ken closed his eyes, took a deep breath, and let out a lengthy sigh.

The collar was up on his brown winter coat, and his navy blue New England Patriots hat was pulled well below his ears.

"Hi, Sweetheart. Cold one today."

Ken had already brushed the snow off of the top of Marie's headstone. The footprints he'd left in the three inches of fresh powder circled the speckled gray stone, which read:

Marie Elaine (Bedell) Roy

Born: June 21, 1953

Left us: December 25, 2017

Loving mother; faithful wife; caring friend

Love Lives On

Some flakes had made their way into the lettering and into the three chiseled tulips above Marie's name. Ken didn't sweep those away, though, because he thought the embedded whiteness looked particularly pretty. He slapped his black finger gloves against his right thigh to knock the snow off. Noticing they were wet, he tucked them under his left armpit before putting his hands in his coat pockets.

"Brooke called last night. She sends her love. She said Celina is starting to sleep through the night. That's good. It's tough getting up in the middle of the night. Remember when we had to do that with Brooke? We used to alternate nights so at least one of us could sleep. Funny, sometimes that seems like a million years ago, and sometimes that feels like yesterday."

Ken tugged his collar higher and made sure his coat zipper was all way to the top. A frigid breeze was giving his exposed neck a chill.

"Hard to believe it's been a week since you left us, Sweetheart. I'm glad Brooke flew here for Thanksgiving. That picture I took of Celina on your lap, I had that framed and put it on your dresser. The girl at the photo place asked me if I wanted anything written on the picture. I didn't know what she meant at first, but then she explained she could type whatever I wanted on the picture, so I had her put 'Grammy loves Celina,' and had her use a heart image for the word 'love,'" explained Ken, moving his index fingers in the shape of a heart. "I think you'd like it.

"Brooke invited me down to her place. That was nice of her. She's on break for a few weeks. I thought about it, but, ahh, well, I didn't want you to be here by yourself."

Ken wiped his nose, which had turned red as the winter breeze stiffened.

"Do you think I made the right decision? It's been eating away at me," said Ken, shaking his head. "I know you couldn't control when you left us; it's not your fault you passed away on Christmas morning. But I just couldn't call Brooke; it was her first Christmas with Celina. I wanted them to enjoy the day. I called first thing the next morning, though. She asked me why I didn't call, and I said you left us really late at night and I didn't want to call and wake Celina. She believed me, but ... but I lied to her about what time her mother died, and I didn't tell her right away that her mother died. I wasn't truthful."

Ken softly kicked his right foot forward, sending the light snow slightly into the air.

"I'm not feeling like a really good father right now."

A gust of wind from the northwest sent a white cloud of snow through the cemetery. Ken pulled his hat down just below his eyebrows.

"Sweetheart, what do you want me to do with your clothes? Brooke said I should give them all to the homeless shelter in Pynchonton, especially since it's winter, but I wanted to ask you first."

Ken lifted his shoulders, his muscles tightening. He tried to blink the water off of his eyelashes.

"I was looking forward to retiring in March, but I'm not so sure now. I think I'm going to get bored. I'm thinking of asking Kevin if I can stay, or maybe stay on part-time. He's already hired someone for my position; someone he went to college with, so I don't know. Do you think I should ask?"

Shivering, Ken slightly bounced on his toes, his arms close to his side.

"I was going to bring some flowers and leave them here, but I figured they'd die ... " Ken stopped abruptly, turning his head briefly away from Marie's headstone. "Ahh, I figured they wouldn't last too long in these conditions. When I come back next week I'll bring something that can hold up in this weather; maybe some winterberries. It might look a little strange, but I know you like winterberries. I could keep them in their pot with some mini pine branches along the bottom. OK? Is that OK with you, Sweetheart?"

Snow began to build at the base of the headstone; the wind was creating a small drift. Trying to fight off the cold, Ken closed his eyes.

Ken reached up, wiping away a bead of sweat from his forehead. He looked to his left, surprised he was this hot in the shade of the oak trees.

"Hi, Rhaymi."

Ken felt uncomfortable, not because he was at a cemetery, but because of the headstone. It was dark and cold and plain – all unlike Rhaymi. He shook his head, dropping it toward the loosened dirt.

"You deserved better. I wish I knew a week ago what I know now."

Ken tapped a small rock out of the way to the right with his foot.

"I could have helped you, but ... but I didn't know ... I didn't know everything. I didn't know what I know now."

Ken rubbed his right hand firmly along his forehead.

"I really need to thank you, Rhaymi. I had a lot of fun spending time with you and having you stay at my house - you calling me 'Old Man.' You were a fun kid; a smart kid. You had a lot going for you.

"And," Ken continued, "you brought me closer to my daughter. For that, I thank you."

His right hand pressed against his lips and down his chin.

"You, ahh, you really opened my eyes; you opened my eyes to a world I really didn't know existed. Yeah, you see things in movies, and maybe see something on the news or read about it in the newspaper. But I never knew anything about abusive relationships. That wasn't part of my life; I didn't think so, anyway. But there it was, with my daughter, right under my roof, and I had no idea."

With his right hand, Ken quickly reached and grabbed the back of his neck, squeezing his skin tightly.

"And then what happened to you. Well, you were such a great kid. My God you had everything going for you. You were in college studying to be a nurse. You were a hard worker and you understood people and you had great energy, and then this happened to you."

Ken wiped his nose with the back of his hand.

"Sorry," he said, taking a deep breath.

He stood motionless for a minute before turning around and looking through the fence at the buildings along the other side of the road.

"I'll be right back."

With purpose he walked out of the cemetery and into a CVS across the street. He returned to Rhaymi's plot five minutes later, holding a plastic bag in his hand.

"Rhay, I don't think I'll be coming back – it's a little too high-end here for me. But, I, ahh … I was wondering if we could do one last thing together before I go?"

Ken reached into the plastic bag and held his hand up. It was a new set of Uno cards.

"I was hoping we could play one last time. OK?"

Ken sat on the dirt, crossing his legs facing the headstone. He unwrapped the plastic on the new deck, leaning to his right to put the wrapper in his left pocket. He pulled the cards out, placed the box in his lap, and began to shuffle.

"OK, this is how we'll play," he explained. "I'm going to deal seven cards, but I'm going to deal them face up. I'll make the best play for both of us. You'll just have to trust me on that. Whoever wins is the Uno champion. Good?"

Ken shuffled a few more times.

"And since we're on your home turf, if a person can't play they just have to draw one card. That should make you happy, Missy Pants."

Leaning forward, Ken dealt the cards face up.

"Good thing it's not windy."

Snapping the last card on the dirt, Ken placed the rest of the cards in the middle, turning over a Green Four.

"OK, you go first."

Inspecting Rhaymi's cards, Ken realized she had a nice string of plays.

"Uh-oh. Looks like you're going to be off to a good start."

Ken played Rhaymi's Green Draw Two, which was her best card. He plucked a Green Eight and a Wild Card off the deck and put them on the dirt next to his left foot.

"OK, not bad. Oh, your roommate took Freddie home. She said she liked Freddie, and her parents have a lot of land so that made sense."

Ken again leaned forward, putting Rhaymi's Green Reverse and Green Nine in the middle, leaving her with four cards compared to his nine.

"Ha, I can hear you now. 'You're going down, Old Man; going down.' You might be right. I'm going to need a big comeback."

Playing his Green Eight, Ken put down Rhaymi's Green Zero and then his Green Two. Raising his eyebrows, Ken put down Rhaymi's Green Five, leaving her with her two cards.

"Not looking good for me."

Ken played his Green One before realizing Rhaymi couldn't play. He slipped a card off the top. It was a Blue Skip.

"That doesn't do you any good now, but that could burn me later. I don't like where this is headed."

Ken played his Red One, changing the game's color for the first time.

"No red; no red for Rhaymi. You'll have to draw."

Dabbing his right index finger with his tongue, Ken grabbed the top card for Rhaymi – a Red Seven.

"You lucky son of a gun," he said, putting the card in the discard pile.

Ken put down his Red Five. He inspected Rhaymi's cards and realized she couldn't play again, so he took a card off the stack. It was a Green Three, which couldn't be played.

"I think the game just turned, my friend."

Ken snapped down his Red Reverse, followed quickly by his Yellow Reverse. Down to two cards, he put his Wild Card on the pile.

"Blue," he said, pointing at the Wild Card.

"Uno."

Ken looked at all of the cards. Rhaymi had four cards left, and he had one. He was going to win.

Slowly, Ken placed Rhaymi's Blue Skip on the pile, and then her Blue Zero. Ken looked at his final card. It was Blue Four. He stared at the card on the ground before looking at Rhaymi's black headstone. He kept his eyes on her middle name: Destiny.

Stretching out his right hand, Ken picked up his remaining card, holding it chest high. He peeked over his Blue Four, looking again at Rhaymi's headstone. He lowered the card, placing it into the right pocket of his jacket.

Ken reached into the plastic CVS bag on the ground. He pulled out a roll of duct tape and a black marker. He stepped forward ripped off an arm's length piece of tape and placed it horizontally on the headstone. He took the cap of the marker off, dropped both knees to the ground and wrote on the tape.

A few seconds later, he stood, putting the tape, marker and plastic bag into his jacket as he backed away from Rhaymi's headstone.

"Did I tell you I'm going to move to Florida? I think I'd like to spend more time with my granddaughter."

Tears filled Ken's eyes.

"Bye, Rhaymi."

Ken turned and walked away from the headstone, which now read:

Rhaymi Destiny Summers

B: August 15, 1998

D: May 17, 2018

UNO QUEEN OF THE WORLD

THE END

Made in the USA
Middletown, DE
01 April 2019